THE PUBLICATIONS COMMITEE OF THE COUNCIL

Twentythird annual report of the Council of Missions

Cooperating with the Church of Christ in Japan

THE PUBLICATIONS COMMITEE OF THE COUNCIL

Twentythird annual report of the Council of Missions
Cooperating with the Church of Christ in Japan

ISBN/EAN: 9783741169236

Manufactured in Europe, USA, Canada, Australia, Japa

Cover: Foto ©Andreas Hilbeck / pixelio.de

Manufactured and distributed by brebook publishing software
(www.brebook.com)

THE PUBLICATIONS COMMITEE OF THE COUNCIL

Twentythird annual report of the Council of Missions

TWENTY-THIRD

ANNUAL REPORT OF THE COUNCIL

OF MISSIONS

COÖPERATING WITH THE

CHURCH OF CHRIST IN JAPAN

ISSUED BY THE PUBLICATIONS COMMITTEE

OF THE COUNCIL

1900

Printed at THE FUKUIN PRINTING COMPANY, L'D.,
Yokohama, Japan.

OFFICERS OF THE COUNCIL
FOR 1900-1901.

PRESIDENT . . T. C. WINN.
VICE PRESIDENT . . E. ROTHESAY MILLER.
SECRETARY . . B. C. HAWORTH.
TREASURER . . JOHN C. BALLAGH.

PUBLICATIONS COMMITTEE.

WILLIAM IMBRIE.

E. ROTHESAY MILLER.

M. N. WYCKOFF.

H. B. PRICE.

H. M. LANDIS.

S. S. SNYDER.

B. C. HAWORTH.

SECRETARIES

CONTENTS.

4. Increase of the salaries of evangelists in special cases.
5. Communication from the Naniwa Presbytery.
6. Sale of the Scriptures.
7. Revision of the Hymnbook.
8. Sunday-school Hymnal and hymns for Christmas and Easter.
9. Replies to resolutions of the last Council memorial of Archdeacon Warren.
10. Resolutions memorial of Mrs. L. H. Pierson.
11. Historical documents.
12. Committee of Arrangements for the next meeting of the Council.
13. General report of the work of next year.
14. Thanks of the Council to the President and request for a copy of his sermon for publication.
15. Thanks to the Karuizawa Church.
16. Appointment of officers and committees.
17. Next annual meeting.
18. Close of the Council.

II. GENERAL REPORT OF THE WORK OF THE YEAR WITH SUPPLEMENT.

III. ROLL OF THE COUNCIL:

1. EAST JAPAN MISSION OF THE PRESBYTERIAN CHURCH IN THE U. S. A. (NORTHERN).
2. WEST JAPAN MISSION OF THE PRESBYTERIAN CHURCH IN THE U. S. A. (NORTHERN).

3. NORTH JAPAN MISSION OF THE REFORMED (Dutch) CHURCH IN AMERICA.
4. SOUTH JAPAN MISSION OF THE REFORMED (Dutch) CHURCH IN AMERICA.
5. MISSION OF THE UNITED PRESBYTERIAN CHURCH OF SCOTLAND.
6. MISSION OF THE PRESBYTERIAN CHURCH IN THE U. S. (SOUTHERN).
7. MISSION OF THE REFORMED (GERMAN) CHURCH IN THE U. S.
8. MISSION OF THE CUMBERLAND PRESBYTERIAN CHURCH.
9. WOMANS UNION MISSIONARY SOCIETY.

I.

PROCEEDINGS

TWENTY-THIRD ANNUAL MEETING
OF THE COUNCIL.

---

1. OPENING AND SESSIONS OF THE COUNCIL.

The Council of Missions Coöperating with the Church of Christ in Japan assembled in the Union Church, Karuizawa, at 10 a.m., July 19th, 1900. The President, the Rev. J. B. Hail, D.D., preached from the text, *Brethren, I count not myself yet to have apprehended: but one thing I do, forgetting the things which are behind, and stretching forward to the things which are before, I press on toward the goal unto the prize of the high calling of God in Christ Jesus. Phil. 3: 12.*

The business meetings each morning were preceded by meetings for prayer conducted by members or corresponding members of the Council. Besides the Sunday services in English and Japanese, two popular meetings were held ; one at 8 p.m. on Friday, the 20th ; and the other at the same hour on Monday, the 23rd. The former meeting was addressed by the Rev. T. M. MacNair, the Rev. H. V. S. Peeke and the Rev. Dr. D. Z. Sheffield, President of Tungchow College; the subject being the Ecumenical Conference held in New York City in April of this year, at which all of the speakers had been present. The meeting on Monday was addressed by Dr. Sheffield on The Transformation of China.

An invitation was extended to all missionaries in Karuizawa to attend the sessions of the Council; and Dr. Sheffield, the Rev. F. Cromer, and the Rev. H. Loomis of the Bible Societies Committee, were invited to sit as corresponding members.

The Rev. T. M. MacNair presented to the Council for the use of its Presidents, a gavel used by him in presiding over one of the sectional meetings of the Ecumenical Conference of Missions held in New York.

The Council continued in session from July 19th to July 23rd.

2. REPORTS OF STANDING COMMITTEES.

Publications Committee

The following report of the Publications Committee* was read and adopted.

Publications

The twenty-second Annual Report of the Council was printed and distributed in the usual manner. A catechism based upon the Confession of Faith of the Church of Christ in Japan, by Dr. Thompson; and also the following tracts by different members of the Council have been published: A Call to the Ministry, by Mr. Pieters; How to Bring Men to Christ, by Dr. J. B. Hail; For One Reading the Gospel, by Mr. Pierson; Faith

---

* Messrs. Imbrie, E. R. Miller, Wyckoff, Price, Landis, Snyder and Haworth.

Establishes the Law, It is finished, Eternal Life, by Mr. Davidson ; *Kirisuto no Kyo*, by Mr. Hudson ; *Kyoikukai ni Okeru Shūkyō no Jiyū* (a tract on education), *Yūsha no Shūkyō* (a tract for soldiers), by Mr. Noss. Light in Darkness (a semi-monthly) by Mr. Jones ; *Yorokobi no Otozure* (a monthly) and *Chiisaki Otozure* (a semi-monthly), by Mrs. E. Rothesay Miller ; and *Nagusame no Kotoba*, by Mr. Hoy, have been issued as usual. Dr. Imbrie has written regularly for the *Fukuin Shimpo* and from time to time for the Expositor. A commentary on the Epistle of James, by Mr. Oltmans ; and one on the First Epistle to the Corinthians, by Dr. Imbrie, are still in preparation.

At the last meeting of the Council the following action was taken regarding the extension of coöperation in the preparation and publication of Sunday-school Literature :— Coöperation in Sunday-school Literature.

Resolved 1. That the Council seconds the action of the Mission of the Methodist Episcopal Church favoring a wider coöperation among the evangelical bodies of Japan in the publication of Sunday-school Literature.

2. That it therefore cordially approves of extending an earnest invitation to the Missions of the American Board and the American Baptist Union to join with it and the Methodist Episcopal Church in this work.

3. That it directs its Publications Committee, in company with the Publications Committee of the Methodist Episcopal Church and with any committees appointed by the Missions of the American Board and the American Baptist Union, to make such changes in the present plan of coöperation as may be rendered necessary by such an extension.

In accordance with these resolutions, the Publications Committee of the Council, the foreign members of the Publications Committee of the Methodist Episcopal Church, together with representatives of the Missions of the American Board and the American Baptist Union, met in the City of Tokyo on September 27th and October 11th 1899, and adopted the following Plan of Coöperation.

1. Each of the coöperating bodies shall appoint biennially two members to serve on a joint committee, which shall be known as the Committee on Sunday-school Literature.

2. The Committee may invite Japanese to sit as associate members.

3. The work of the Committee shall be the preparation of the following publications, as aids to the study of the International Lessons :

    a. A SUNDAY-SCHOOL MONTHLY for the use of teachers and advanced students. This shall include two parts ;* the second to contain exegetical notes especially intended for those who desire to make a more thorough study of the text.

    b. A SUNDAY-SCHOOL QUARTERLY prepared particularly for the use of pupils from the Primary Schools (Sho-gakko).

    c. A BEGINNERS LEAFLET designed for the youngest pupils.

4. It is intended that these publications shall be available for all the Evangelical Churches in Japan ; and they shall be prepared in accordance with that purpose.

5. The representatives of the several coöperating bodies shall have an equal voice in the management of affairs ; and any deficit shall be apportioned in equal parts among the coöperating bodies.

6. The publication and distribution of the work of the Committee shall be in charge of the Methodist Publishing House, which shall also employ a translator approved by the Committee, and to whom members of the Committee may send their work on the publications for translation.

7. The Committee shall appoint a Chairman and Secretary ; stated meetings shall be held as the Committee may appoint ; special meetings shall be held at the request

---

* See the report of the Committee on Sunday-school Literature, page 5.

of any two members. The Committee shall prepare an annual report to be presented to the several coöperating bodies.

8. Any one of the coöperating bodies desiring to withdraw shall give to the Committee formal notice to that effect six months prior to withdrawal.

9. This plan of coöperation may be amended by a two-thirds vote of all the members of the Committee.

The Committee or Sunday-school Literature representing the four coöperating bodies is now composed of the following persons : From this Council, Messrs. H. M. Landis and F. S. Scudder ; from the Methodist Episcopal Church, Messrs. B. Chappell and G. F. Draper ; from the Mission of the American Board, Dr. George Albrecht and Miss G. Cozad ; from the Mission of the American Baptist Union, Mr. F. G. Harrington and Mrs. R. A. Thompson.

Regarding the preparation of a course of study for pastors and evangelists and the establishing of a circulating library (or libraries) for the benefit of pastors and evangelists, the Publications Committee has as yet taken no action.

The following report of the Committee on Sunday-school Sunday-schoo Literature Literature was presented by Mr. Landis and adopted.

The report of the Publications Committee as already presented contains an account of the reorganization of the Committee on Sunday-school Literature so as to include representatives from the Mission of the American Board and from that of the American Baptist Union. At the suggestion of some of the Japanese brethren, the division of the MONTHLY into two separate parts* was given up ; and it was also decided that the text be inserted verse by verse, as commented upon in the exegesis of each passage. The Committee earnestly requests the members of the Council to increase by every means in their power the circulation of the various publications, as well as to make

---

* See 3. a. page 4.

such suggestions to the Japanese workers as shall enable them to make the best use of them.

The report included also a statement of the number of the several publications issued, together with their prices. During the last half of this year the work of preparing the MONTHLY will fall chiefly upon Mr. Landis.

Statistics The Committee on Statistics* presented its report which was adopted. The following is summary of it. The educational and evangelistic work, to which reference is made in the paragraphs immediately below, is work directly under the care of the Coöperating Missions.

EDUCATIONAL WORK :—Theological schools, 2; theological students, 18; Bible women students, 24;† boarding schools for boys, 3; pupils in the same, 322; boarding schools for girls, 11; pupils in the same, 721; day schools, 13; pupils in the same, 1159; foreign teachers, (men) 11, (women) 32; Japanese teachers, (men) 85+, (women) 79+; amount granted by the Boards of Foreign Missions for educational work, yen 37873.†

EVANGELISTIC WORK :—Japanese ordained ministers, 34; salaries of the same, yen 9415; unordained evangelists, 113; salaries of the same, yen 22591; Bible women,† 56+; amount granted by the Boards of Foreign Missions for evangelistic work yen 39179.†

Number of missionaries, 150; stations where missionaries reside, 36; outstations, 160.

---

* Messrs. Landis, Noss, Winn, Pieters and Curtis.

† The Bible Womans Institute of the Womans Union Missionary Society also reports 95 women in Bible work or training. As the Council has received no financial statistics from the Mission of this Society, the amounts given as granted by the Boards of Foreign Missions both for educational and for evangelistic work should be increased by the amount expended through this Mission.

The tables on the following pages were prepared by the Committee on Statistics from the reports of the Presbyteries.‡

	TOTALS				AVERAGE PER COMMUNICANT.		
PRESBYTERY	No. of communicants	Added on confession	Sunday-school members	Contributions	Contributions to Board of Home Missions†	Contributions to all objects
				Yen.		*Yen.*
Tokyo	4979	256	1771	12007.35	.08½	2.47
Miyagi	1654	177	1438	3496.22	.08¾	2.11
Naniwa	3151	200	2071	8538.69	.10¾	2.71
Sanyo	372	30	285	1223.64	?	3.29
Chinzei	642	37	342	1368.45	.21	2.13
Totals or general averages	10798	700	5907	26634.35	.09⅘	2.47

PRESBYTERY	Ordained ministers	Unordained evangelists	Advisory members
Tokyo	31	50	3
Miyagi	17	13	6
Naniwa	17	17	13
Sanyo	10	10	0
Chinzei	6	19	4
Totals	81	109	26

* A yen is half a dollar in gold.

† The Synod does not meet until October of this year, eighteen months after its last meeting. The statistics in this table are taken from the reports to the Presbyteries, which do not exhibit the contributions made *directly* to the Board of Home Missions by members of the churches. A calculation including these gifts would very greatly raise the average per member. The receipts reported at the last meeting of the Synod were *yen* 2759.

* For the sake of missionaries coöperating with the Church of Christ in Japan, but who are unable to enter Presbyteries in the usual way by letters of dismission from the other Presbyteries, the following provision is made:—Canon 21 6. Advisory Members: Ministers who sincerely accept the Constitution, Canons and Confession of Faith, and who statedly coöperate in the work of the Church of Christ in Japan, but who are unable to apply for admission under Canon 14, may be admitted as Advisory Members by a two-thirds vote. Advisory Members may speak, introduce resolutions, and be elected to serve on committees. But no committee shall have a majority of Advisory Members. Presbyteries having four or less than four Advisory Members shall elect one to sit as an Advisory Member of the Synod. Those having eight shall elect two; those having twelve, three.

SUMMARY BY PRESBYTERIES

INCREASE

PRESBYTERIES	No. of members at end of 1898	Baptisms			Baptized in Infancy and admitted to the Lord's Table			Restored			Received by letter		
		M.	W.	C.	M.	W.	C.	M.	W.	C.	M.	W.	C.
Tokyo	4927	121	112	57	6	17	...	1	1	...	85	64	23
Miyagi	1681	117	52	10	4	7	...	...	...	...	65	48	12
Naniwa	2909	100	83	51	6	11	...	...	...	...	66	73	19
Sanyo	473*	15	15	14	...	...	...	...	...	...	16	...	...
Chinzei . . .	632*	20	11	14	2	1	...	2	1	...	...	29	11
Total . . .	10622	373	276	...	18	33	...	4	2	...	232	205	65

DECREASE

	Dismissions by letter			Deaths			Exclusions			Names erased from the register			No. of members at end of 1899			
	M.	W.	C.	M.	W.	C.	M.	W.	C.	M.	W.	C.	M.	W.	C.	Total.
Tokyo	63	81	34	32	31	2	4	1	...	93	71	43	2105	2213	663	4979
Miyagi	66	38	6	15	11	1	5	1	6	99	77	2	951	581	102	1654
Naniwa	41	55	27	20	15	...	33	5	...	21	9	1	1348	1301	482	3151
Sanyo	...	...	...	...	...	...	...	...	...	...	...	...	...	...	...	372
Chinzei . . .	28	26	17	2	1	...	7	2	...	35	37	14	259	263	149	642
Total . . .																10798

* From the table of last year. † The number of adult converts baptized added to that of those baptized in infancy and admitted to the Lord's Table is 700.

9

SUMMARY BY PRESBYTERIES
(Continued)

PRESBYTERIES	Attendance at Sunday service			Attendance at prayer meeting			Residence changed but known			Residence not known			Ceased to commune		
	M.	W.	Total.	M.	W.	Total.	M.	W.	C.	M.	W.	C.	M.	W.	C.
Tokyo . . .	715	718	1433	311	278	589	701	601	128	92	74	2	24	15	...
Miyagi . . .	...	...	722	...	...	...	242	142	19	13	2	...	12	6	...
Naniwa . . .	583	609	1192	236	235	481	574	452	113	24	13	...	5	2	...
Sanyo . . .	...	...	316	...	...	...	...	...	...	...	...	...	...	...	...
Chinzei . . .	...	...	...	...	...	...	79	79	34	6	4	...	7	4	...

	SUNDAY-SCHOOLS						CONTRIBUTIONS				
	Children		Adults		Teachers		Congregational expenses	Contributions for evangelistic work	Total contributions	Pastors or evangelists	Elders
	Boys	Girls	M.	W.	M.	W.					
Tokyo . . .	542	706	159	176	99	89	Yen. 11604.79	402.56	12007.35	38	150
Miyagi . . .	536	696	78	33	57	38	3352.74	143.48	3496.22	32	25
Naniwa . . .	619	701	293	285	80	93	8197.86	340.83	8538.69	34	52
Sanyo . . .	71*	71	72	67	17	... 6	...	...	1223.64	...	...
Chinzei . . .	934	93	66		17		1233.29	135.16	1368.45	11	17
Total . . .	1861	2267	667	633	333	226			26634.35		

* The report from the Sanyo Presbytery gives only the total 256; that from Chinzei gives 196 children and 133 adults. It will be seen that there are in all 1495 teachers and 5428 scholars.

10

The Committee on Self-support* reported that it had Self-support been thought unnecessary to present a detailed report at this meeting of the Council.

The Treasurer of the Council presented the Financial Finances of the Council Report for the year. The report was referred to the Auditing Committee †, who examined the same together with the vouchers and reported it correct. The report was then adopted.

3. REPORT OF SPECIAL COMMITTEES APPOINTED BY THE LAST COUNCIL.

The General Report of the Work of the Year‡ was read General Report of the Work of the Year by Miss Deyo. A resolution was adopted thanking Miss Deyo for her excellent report, and directing that it be printed.

The Rev. W. Y. Jones, Chairman of the Committee on Expansion of work Expansion§ presented the following report which was adopted.

The Committee appointed by the last Council to consider the need of expanding the work of the Coöperating Missions, and also to urge upon the Home Boards and Churches the need of increased funds as well as of more workers, both Japanese and foreign, would respectfully make the following report :—

The Committee was composed of Messrs. W. Y. Jones, F. S. Scudder, W. E. Hoy, A. Oltmans and H. B. Price. Mr. Hoy was unable to be present at the meetings of the Committee but approved of the results of its deliberations.

---

* Messrs. Oltmans, Price and Jones.
† Messrs. Scudder and Wyckoff.
‡ See II following the Proceedings of the Council.
§ Messrs. Jones, Scudder, Hoy, Oltmans and Price.

A letter was prepared for the home Churches, and copies were sent to all of the Missions of the Council and to all the Boards with which the several Missions are connected. Accompanying the copies sent to the various Missions was a note embodying the three following recommendations: 1. That each Mission also send the letter of the Committee to its own Board, endorsing it and accompanying it with a letter of its own. 2. That each Mission take into consideration the feasibility of a closer and more vital union of the Coöperating Missions, looking to some more effective method of fully occuping the fields now under the care of the Missions and also the fields contemplated in the method of expansion proposed by the committee. 3. That any action or suggestions along this line be sent to the Chairman of the Committee to be reported to the next meeting of the Council.

Besides this, a list of twenty places not yet occupied by members of the Coöperating Missions, was prepared. These points, fourteen of which have no resident missionaries of any Church, would if occupied make an almost continuous line of work from the Hokkaidō to the south of Kyūshū.

The action of all of the Missions has not been reported; but at least four have sent the letter of the Committee to their respective Boards reënforcing it by letters of their own.

The German Reformed and West Japan Presbyterian Missions have signified their intention of locating missionaries as soon as possible in the places suggested by the Committee. All of the Missions have not replied regarding the number of new missionaries asked for as reënforcements; but the Cumberland Presbyterian Mission is asking for six families and twelve single ladies; the West Japan Mission for four families and one single lady; the East Japan Mission for two families and five single ladies; and the North Japan Mission of the Reformed (Dutch) Church for two families and two single ladies.

The Committee in suggesting to the various Missions unoccupied points which the Coöperating Missions would do

well to enter, referred the places in the Hokkaido to the
East Japan Presbyterian Mission. The German Reformed
Mission however has made a request to the Committee
that it be given one point in the Hokkaido since it has
already had some connection with that field. This request
having been received only recently, the Committee felt that
it could not adjust the matter before this meeting the
Council and recommends that the matter be referred to
the German Reformed and East Japan Presbyterian
Missions.

The Committee discussed the feasibility of some closer
and more vital union of the Coöperating Missions looking
to some more effective method of fully occupying the fields
now under the care of the Missions, and also the fields contemplated in the method of expansion which the committee
has proposed; but nothing practical was agreed upon, nor
has any one of the Missions made any such suggestions.
The Committee therefore refers this question back to the
Council, hoping that it may be able to devise some method
that will meet the needs of the case.

Following is the list of places suggested by the Committee (the Liu Chu Islands having been added by the
Council) for the location of additional missionaries.

Hokkaidō (Yeso): two places not yet named. West
Coast: Akita, Tsurugaoka or Sakata, Niigata, Takata,
Toyama. Northern Japan: Ichinoseki, Taira, Koriyama,
Shirakawa or Fukushima. Central Japan: Oyama, Kofu,
Matsumoto, Iida, Takayama. Kyūshū: Nakatsu, Kuma-
moto. Islands: Tsushima, Goto Islands, Liu Chu Is-
lands.

Of the above places the following have resident missionaries belonging to other Churches. The remainder have
no resident missionaries.

Place	Mission	No. of Families.	Single Ladies
Akita	Christian	One	—
Niigata	A. B. C. F. M.	„	Two
Matsumoto	S. P. G.	„	One
Takayama	Scandanavian	„	--
Nakatsu	M. E. (South)	„	—
Kumamoto	C. M. S.	„	Two

The report of the Committee on Ministerial Relief*
was presented by Dr. M. N. Wyckoff. The Council accepted the report, requested the Committee to continue
for another year, to give the matter further consideration,
and to report at the next meeting of the Council.

The report of the Committee on the Training of Lay
Workers was presented by Mr. Winn. The Council
adopted the report along with the following statement and
resolution :

"Recognizing the latent power in the churches which
ought to be awakened and called into service, and believ-
ing that much profit will come from knowing what is
being done and with what success to lead Christians to
feel and discharge their responsibility for giving the gospel
to those about them—
Resolved : That a committee† be appointed to gather
information and report as to the methods used and success
attained in enlisting and guiding laymen in local evangelistic work connected with their own churches.

4. NEW BUSINESS.

A committee‡ was appointed to express to the Board
of Foreign Missions of the Free United Presbyterian
Church of Scotland the appreciation by the Council of
the work of the Mission of the U. P. Church in Japan,
and to urge that the Mission be continued and reënforced.

A committee§ consisting of one member from each
Mission connected with the Council was appointed to

---

* Messrs. Pieters, Wyckoff and J. B. Hail.
† Messrs. S. P. Fulton, M. N. Wyckoff and J. C. Ballagh.
‡ Messrs. Imbrie, E. S. Booth and T. C. Winn.
§ Messrs. MacNair, Winn, E. Rothesay Miller, Peeke, S. P. Fulton,
Schneder and J. B. Hail.

consider the possibility of a better distribution of the forces of the Coöperating Missions.

The committee* appointed to prepare a statement Reënforcements setting forth to the Boards represented in the Council the need of reënforcing the Missions presented its report. During its consideration a number of suggestions were made that seemed likely to have weight; and the report was referred to the Publications Commitee for further consideration and transmission to the Boards.

The following resolution adopted by the North Japan Increase of salaries of evangelists in certain cases Mission of the Reformed Church and concurred in by the East Japan Mission of the Presbyterian Church was received by the Council and by it referred to the Coöperating Missions for their consideration.

Resolved : That the Mission adopts the general principle that marked efficiency and fidelity on the part of an evangelist, or the existence of circumstances that are evidently exceptional, shall justify the Mission in increasing his salary to such an extent as shall seem proper to the Mission after a careful consideration by it of the facts in each individual case.

A communication having been received from the Naniwa Communication from Naniwa Presbytery Presbytery on the subject of an increase of the scale of salaries paid by the Coöperating Missions to evangelists, the Council instructed the Secretary to communicate to the Presbytery its action in regard to the above resolution adopted by the North Japan Mission of the Reformed Church and concurred in by the East Japan Mission of the Presbyterian Church.

---

* Messrs. Brokaw and E. Rothesay Miller.

The Rev. H. Loomis of the Bible Societies Committee and the Rev. S. S. Snyder addressed the Council on the sale of the Scriptures by missionaries. A resolution was adopted cordially commending such work.

Mr. MacNair made a statement regarding the work of the Committee of the Synod on the Revision of the Hymnbook, and also read a letter from the Rev. Geo. Allchin in reference to a proposed union hymnbook. The subject was referred to a committee;* and after further consideration by the Council no action was taken.

The Council having learned of the preparation of a Sunday-school Hymnal by Mrs. Jones and Miss Glenn, expressed its high appreciation of the value of such a book. It also directed that a service for Easter prepared by Mr. Scudder and one for Christmas prepared by Mrs. MacNair be referred to the Publications Committee for publication, and that the Committee on Sunday-school Literature be recommended to insert them at the proper time in the Sunday-school Quarterly.

The following letters addressed to the Secretary in reply to the resolutions of the Council regarding the late Arch-deacon Warren were read.

Karuizawa, July 29th, 1899.

Dear Sir :

Please accept my warm thanks for the very kind expression of sympathy which I have received from the Council of Missions regarding my dear husband. It

---

* Messrs. MacNair and Peeke.

16

certainly is gratifying to know how warmly he was appreciated by all bodies of Christians.

With kind regards, believe me,

Yours sincerely,

L. WARREN.

Osaka, August 22nd, 1899.

Dear Sir :

I am instructed by the Standing Sub-committee of the C. M. Society for this jurisdiction, to convey to the Council of Coöperating Missions through you their gratitude for the kind resolution of sympathy so kindly sent, and to say that the same is being forwarded to London.

Believe me, Yours truly,

C. THEO. WARREN.

Acting SEC., C. M. Soc.

The following resolutions in memory of the late Mrs. L. H. Pierson were presented by the committee* appointed to prepare them, and were adopted by the Council.

Whereas, in the unerring providence of the Great Head of the Church, He has been pleased to call away by death, at Yokohama, on November 28th, 1899, one of the foremost woman missionary workers of the world, a representative of the Womans Union Missionary Society of America and a member of this Council.

Resolved: That, as the Council of the Coöperating Missions we hereby express our sympathy with the Mission and the Society with which our esteemed fellow-worker was so long connected, and that we also express our gratitude to the Lord of the harvest for having commissioned and sustained so long in her unsparing labors so admirably equipped and so eminently successful a laborer in educational and evangelistic work; in both of which she was eminently blessed.

---

* Messrs. J. H. Ballagh and Booth.

Resolved: That in Mrs. Pierson's catholicity of spirit and ardent attachment to her Lord and Saviour, as well as in her loving sympathy with all classes of the people, we find an inspiration to seek the same conformity to Christ and a like devotion to the salvation of men.

Resolved: That we record our thanks for the important services Mrs. Pierson's labors have rendered to the Church of Christ in Japan, in training up teachers, Bible women, and those who have become wives of pastors and Christian laymen, and in her direct evangelistic work extending to a large part of the field occupied by members of this Council; and that we crave earnestly the blessing of God upon her successor in the care of this important work, and upon the multitudes of those who directly or indirectly have been brought under the influence of Mrs. Pierson's devoted example and labors.

Resolved: That a copy of these resolutions be forwarded to the Secretaries of the Mission and Board of the W. U. M. S., and to the papers of the Churches represented in this Council.

Historical documents The Secretary of Council, the Librarian of the Meiji Gakuin and Dr. Imbrie were constituted a committee to to collect and hold copies of all the Annual Reports of the Council and other documents of historical value to the Council and the Church of Christ in Japan.

Committee of Arrangements Messrs. Landis and Booth were appointed the Committee of Arrangements for the next meeting of the Council.

Report of Work of the Year Dr. J. B. Hail was appointed to prepare the next General Report of the Work of the Year.

Thanks of the Council to the President The thanks of the Council were returned to Dr. J. B. Hail, the retiring President, for his faithful and efficient services; and he was requested to offer a copy of his sermon to the *Fukuin Shimpo* for publication.

The thanks of the Council were returned to the Karni- zawa Church for the use of its building and other courtesies.

On the recommendation of the Committee on Nomina- tions, the following appointments for the coming year were made.

President, T. C. Winn; Vice President, E. Rothesay Miller; Secretary, B. C. Haworth; Treasurer, J. C. Ballagh.

Publications Committee: William Imbrie, E. Rothesay Miller, M. N. Wyckoff, H. B. Price, H. M. Landis, S. S. Synder and B. C. Haworth.

Committee on Distribution of Forces: T. M. MacNair, T. C. Winn, E. Rothesay Miller, H. V. S. Peeke, S. P. Fulton, D. B. Schneder and J. B. Hail.

Committee on Statistics: C. Noss, H. M. Landis, T. C. Winn, A. Pieters and F. S. Curtis.

The Council adjourned to meet in Karuizawa, at 10 a.m., on the second Thursday of August, 1901.

After singing a hymn, the Council closed with prayer and the benediction by the President, the Rev. T. C. Winn.

II.

GENERAL REPORT OF THE WORK OF THE YEAR

BY

Miss Deyo.

A backward look

This being the last Council report of the century, it seems almost inevitable that we should lift up our heads from the present work for a moment and turn for a long look back. There is much to cheer us in this far backward look over the forty-one years of mission work in Japan. Very much has been attempted, very much has been accomplished. The progress which seemed so painful so slow as, each absorbed in his own work, we glanced over any one year's successes and failures, stands out in grand proportions now, when we view it as a whole. The discouragements and reverses, so harassing to the individual worker, sink into to insignificance, as we see the large results attained in the aggregate.

For while the tired waves vainly breaking
  Seem here no painful inch to gain,
Far back through creek and inlet making,
  Comes silent flooding in the main.

And not by eastern windows only,
  When daylight comes, comes in the light ;
In front, the sun climbs slow, how slowly :
  But backward look ! the land is bright.

20

Even so is the coming of the kingdom. And, as in this land, where forty years ago there was no knowledge of Jehovah or His gospel, where there was nothing but hatred and fear of the religion of Christ, we now see 440 organized Protestant churches, with 42000 communicants, with over 700 missionaries and 800 Japanese ministers and evangelists, with 160 mission schools with over 12000 pupils, with the whole Bible and abundance of Christian literature ready to put in the hand of the inquirer, with every obstacle to the free and full teaching of the gospel in every corner of the land taken away, and a spirit of inquiry gradually permeating the mass of the people, we lift up grateful praise to the conquering Captain of our Salvation, and turn back to our work with glad courage. And this, while we know there are yet 45 millions who are not Christians—a thousand heathen to each believer; that 40 millions have as yet no knowledge whatever, or at best but a vague inkling of what Christianity means, that Buddhism, aroused and fighting for its life, is able yet to prejudice millions against the "evil religion;" that materialism and worldliness have increased with the advance of civilization; and the lust of the flesh, the lust of the eyes, and the pride of life rage rampant through the land. It is n..t because the battle is nearly done that we take courage, but because it is well begun.

Forty years ago, with dangers and restrictions on every side, among people strongly hostile to foreigners and authorities bitterly opposed to Christianity, with scarcely any one able to communicate with them, without dictionary grammar or phrase-book, the first missionaries began prospecting and preparing.

At the end of a decade, there were Dr. Hepburn's English-Japanese and Japanese-English Dictionary, a romanized phrase-book and a few other helps to the study of the language. Many Bibles and tracts in Chinese had been circulated. A few tracts had been prepared in Japanese and Bible translation was well begun. And, most of all, prejudice had been greatly lessened in higher circles and a spirit of inquiry concerning Christianity had been awakened. Much English had been taught and some private Bible classes carried on.

Second decade 1870-1880 A time of organizing During the next decade, over 30 churches were organized and at least 10 schools established. In 1877, the union of the Presbyterial Churches was effected, the autonomy of the Church begun, and this Council of the Coöperating Missions established. The Union Bible Translation Committee was organized, and the New Testament was put to press. The statistics of 1880 report 122 missionaries on the field and about 3000 Christians.

Third decade 1880-1890 Time of greatest advance Between 1880 and 1890 was the time of greatest advancement. Then the people flocked in hundreds to hear Christian lectures; churches and preaching places were crowded; and numbers were added to the Church almost daily. Mission schools, though increased in numbers and greatly enlarged in size, were all filled to overflowing. The country seemed bent on adopting everything foreign; and hopes were entertained by many that by the end of the century, it would no longer be necessary to send new missionaries to Japan. The statistics for 1890 were 577 missionaries occupying 43 places; 423 outstations where there were no missionaries; 297 organized churches (54 of them self-supporting) with 32000 members; and 584 ministers and evangelists.

Fourth decade Confusion obstruction Then suddenly came a period of confusion and obstruction. The cart was going so fast that it got ahead of the horses. In the nation, a reaction against foreign influence came in like a flood. In the Church, intellectualism was rampant, and there was a craze for modern thought and the very latest scientific theories. An idea that was more than a year old was liable to be slighted as out of date, and the very name of the *Old* Testament was taken as an indication that to read it would be a waste of time. The air was thick with schemes and plans for church and mission work, but there seemed to be no one to work the plans. Fine organizations sprang up with heads a plenty and to spare, but the other organs were sadly lacking. Long-headed and well-equipped leaders stood around in each other's way, a drug on the market; but followers were rare and at a premium.

22

There was a great falling off in attendance at the churches, and the faith of many waxed cold.

In mission affairs, problems piled up on top of each other; and as some one expressed it, "a condition of crisis was chronic." Self-support and coöperation were household words; the question of foreign or Japanese control of mission schools and mission funds vibrated the air. It was an era of councils and conferences and committees. It was also an era of "cuts." For the Coöperating Missions, the convention held at Kobe in 1893 cleared up some confusion; and some hitherto vague ideas were crystalized into shape: so that, though the chief questions of that conference, viz., What is the proper policy of coöperation? and, Are more missionaries needed? were not answered then, the discussion marked a turning point, which progressing in the new direction found expression in 1897 in the adoption of the resolution that "coöperation is, in the opinion of the Council, best carried out where the Japanese Church organization, in its Sessions, Presbyteries and Synod, directs all ecclesiastical matters, availing itself of the counsels and assistance of the Missions and missionaries as occasion arises; while the Missions direct their own educational, evangelistic and other missionary operations, availing themselves likewise of whatever counsel and assistance they may be able to obtain from their brethren in the Japanese Church:" and in 1899, in a resolution emphasizing the need of an increase of the missionary force, and appointing a committee to especially and specifically present this need to the attention of the home Boards. The schools also passed from one problem and crisis to another. The various surprises sprung upon them by changing outward conditions being climaxed by the now famous "Instruction" of the Minister of Education, promulgated last July. And in addition to all the "fightings without and fears within," consequent upon conditions in this country, we had also to bear the anxiety and distress caused by the falling off in the contributions in the home Churches, which made it inevitable that much promising work should be cut off or neglected, and was the occasion of the withdrawal of many of the

23

best trained workers from the work of the Church, where they had been educated, into other occupations where they could receive higher salaries.

Striking statistics

On the whole, the decade from which we are now emerging, while doubtless a time of growth in wisdom, and perchance in grace, both on the part of the Missions and the Church, has not been a time of much advance. The statistics for 1900 are 727 missionaries occupying 66 places; 827 outstations; 444 organized churches (83 of them self-supporting) with 41800 members; and 837 ministers and evangelists. The most striking point in these statistics is that, while between 1880 and 1890 the number of Christians was multiplied by 10, an increase of 1000%; between 1890 and 1900 the increase was only 25%.

Some problems settled

But the problems are less pressing than they were. One after another has been in a measure solved, or in a manner laid aside. Some organizations have slipped out of existence and large far-reaching plans are less in evidence. There has been a gradual settling down to an acceptance of the fact that spiritual husbandry, like literal, must be accomplished in the sweat of the brow of the individual workers; that there is no royal road to evangelization; but that Poor Richard's maxim, "He who by the plough would thrive, himself must either hold or drive," applies to the Lord's vineyard also. So while there has been a steady advance in comity and confederation, there is also a strengthening conviction that the work for which we have come, can be best accomplished, after a due division of labor has been made, by each Mission and each missionary giving his own direct, personal, continuous attention to the work with which he has been entrusted. Some sentences from Mr. Speer's admirable report come in fitly here as expressing the views now prevailing. " I believe there is a need of keeping our mission ranks full of men who will go out among the people—the choicest men to be found. Missionaries will be needed for a long time to come, to build up, to enlarge, to buttress and train and ballast the churches, to preach the gospel to the poor and the rich, in season and out of season, in the home, by the wayside. Forty millions are ready and waiting to hear. The work needed is down among the foundations. It may not be much known, but it will be laid into that corner stone which abides.

The few events of the past year requiring special notice are more or less connected with the working of the new treaties, which went into effect just before the Council meeting of last year. The government and officials have done their best to make the new laws and regulations work smoothly. The proclamations of H. M. the Emperor and the Ministers of State and Education had their due effect upon popular feeling; and the public generally is ready to "associate cordially with peoples from afar:" while the strict injunction to school children to stop their rudeness to foreigners has had a most salutary effect.

Some free-born Americans have felt annoyed at the tiresome red-tape-ism of the registering and reporting of past history now required; and there have been some warmly contested points concerning the application of the tax laws to certain conditions; and some protesting against certain judgments given in the lower courts: but, on the whole, the great change in Japan's relations to foreign nations has been affected without jar or untoward occurrence. Japan's Ship of State yields easily to the helm; and, as in the case of the change from an autocratic to a constitutional government, and from a silver to a gold standard, the change of course has been accomplished almost without attracting the attention of the passengers.

Since the issuing of the Notification Regarding the Propagation of Religion, Christianity is receiving government recognition; and, in a way, sanction. The strong efforts made by the priests to have Buddhism acknowledged as the national religion not only failed signally; but this failure was followed by the government's introducing into the Diet a bill to place all religions on the same footing before the law. Owing to the strong pressure

25

brought to bear upon members of the Diet by the Buddhist hierarchy, the bill was defeated; but it is believed a similar one will be introduced at the next session. In the midst of this agitation, Shintoism which, being the religion of the Emperor and the court, was supposed to have the best claim to be considered the state religion, has quietly retired. It requested and received official permission to announce that Shinto is not a religion but a cult; a system of rites to be performed in memory of former sovereigns of the empire. The move is significant, as it leaves the Emperor and the court without any religion.

Religious questions have been more discussed in public circles and the public press this year than ever before. The great and growing immorality of the nation, and especially of the young men, causes much anxiety to all thoughtful patriots : and the necessity of some religion is more generally acknowledged in higher circles than it was some years ago. Some are still bombastically asserting that none of the old religions are good enough for the New Japan. She must compile one for herself, or wait for some new leader ; but many are turning to investigate Christianity in the spirit of John the Baptist's question, "Art thou he that should come, or look we for another?" May the missionaries and the Church be ready to answer it in the way Christ did! Not by arguments, nor philosophy, nor even by theology, will such be convinced. Not by treatises and reasoning can we best prove that there is life in the seed ; but by planting it in human hearts that the life may manifest itself.

The general features of the work carried on by the Council, as reported by the Missions composing it, contain nothing of special prominence. On the whole, the work has gone on much as in the previous year. Though at first it was feared that the "Instruction" of the Minister of Education, forbidding religious teaching or worship in schools having government recognition, would be a serious blow to mission schools, only two of our primary schools have been given up; and though others have lost in numbers, the missionaries in charge have found compensations, and feel that on the whole the work of the year has been satisfactory.

We begin our summary of the reports with that of the South Japan Mission, R. C. A. (Dutch) which occupies Kyūshyū, and was established in 1859.

Four families, one single man and four single women South Japan Mission of the R.C.A. (Dutch) compose the Mission. Of these, the Rev. and Mrs. H. V. S. Peeke and Miss Couch have been in America all year. The Rev. Mr. Myers came out in September and has taught English in the boys school in Nagasaki; thus relieving the Rev. Mr. Pieters who removed with his family to Kagoshima, where he gave his time to the study of the language until March, when they went to America on furlough. Dr. Stout took the principalship of the school in Mr. Pieter's place, and has taught in the school and had charge of the Nagasaki station and its 3 out-stations, none of which are more than a day's journey away. Miss Stryker and Miss Stout are also in Nagasaki in charge of the girls schools. The Rev. and Mrs. A. Oltmans are in Saga in charge of that station and its nine outstations, 3 of which are a day's journey away, and 3 more than a day's journey away. Miss Lansing has spent the year in Kagoshima studying the language; but she has also had three Sunday-schools and done some English teaching. Kagoshima with its five outstations is Mr. Peeke's station. During his absence, the Japanese pastor, Mr. Murakata, has looked after the field as well as he could.

The Mission employs 4 ordained ministers and 12 Japanese assistants licensed evangelists, 2 of whom are graduates of the Academic Course of a mission school; 19 school teachers, and one Bible woman who gives part of her time to teaching in the school. It has expended *yen* 5848 for evangelistic work, and *yen* 4645 for educational work.

The girls school, Sturges Seminary, has had a year's Sturges Seminary uninterrupted prosecution of work on the usual lines, and is in a good condition every way. The course of study is six years long. Graduates from the government Higher

27

Primary Schools can enter the first year of the course. The school has a Japanese principal who does his full share of class room work. Miss Stryker, in addition to teaching, has the entire charge of the home department, as she is the only missionary living in the school; though Miss Stout does much class room work. There was an average attendance during the year of 58, about 30 of whom were boarders. In April, 4 were graduated from the advanced course, 3 from the general course, and 2 from the sewing course. The first 7 are Christians. Last year, the ladies were troubled over the lack of spiritual interest in the school, but now the condition is much better. In the fall, a Christian Endeavor Society was started, and has proved a very helpful organization. Through its prayer meetings and committee work, the girls' spiritual life is strengthened, and they are receiving training in religious work. There have been 4 baptisms since last May, and there are now 13 Christians in school. The school is 13 years old. Of the 29 graduates, one is in evangelist work under mission direction, and one is teaching in a mission school. The cost of the school to the Mission, exclusive of missionaries' salaries, is *yen* 2697. Both ladies have studied the language, and Miss Stout has taken her first examination.

Steele College

The boys high school, called Steele College, has undergone some changes in methods, necessitated by a change in the teaching force; but the course of study, so far as there were classes to take it, was taught regularly throughout the year. There was no Junior Class. This course also consists of six years, receiving pupils from the government Higher Primary Schools. There were 85 pupils in school during the year, chiefly in the three lower classes. Dr. Stout says, "The college was, therefore, more than ever a sort of preparatory school, preparing for nothing in particular. This is a condition of things experienced very much in common with other schools of its class, to be accounted for largely from the fact that the government is doing so much for education that the inducements offered by mission schools are little beyond that of efficiency in furnishing students

28

with a practical knowledge of the English language. When this is supposed to be accomplished, the pupils leave to engage in business, or to study elsewhere, where they can escape conscription and receive diplomas of recognized value." Plans are now in contemplation to make the school course five years, and more nearly equivalent to the government Middle School course than at present. There were no graduates at the last commencement. Last year the spiritual condition of the school left much to be desired. The opening of the school year in September found only 3 Christian students on the rolls, and no marked leaning toward Christianity on the part of the students, though there were a number of pupils, some from Christian homes, whose morals were exemplary and influence salutary. During the year, there has been an increase in religious interest on the part of the body of students, and 3 more have united with the Church; so there are now 6 Christian students. One great defect of the school is its lack of teachers of pronounced Christian character. Four of the nine teachers are Christians; one a graduate of the school. The school is 13 years old. Of the 25 graduates, 4 are in evangelistic work in the employ of Mission. The cost of the school to the Mission last year was *yen* 2670, a great reduction from previous years. This reduction was made necessary by a " cut," and possible by the giving of more missionary time to the school to take the place of the extra foreign teacher previously engaged, and the dismissal of a high salaried Japanese teacher.

In the report of the evangelistic work, 4 churches are mentioned. Evangelistic work The one at Nagasaki reports some baptisms, including 2 Normal School students; 10 candidates for baptism, and an increase of *yen* 120 in contributions. The church is self-supporting, in that it pays all incidental expenses and *yen* 20 a month salary to the Rev. Mr. Segawa. Many members have been dropped from the rolls; some because of removal, and some through discipline. The work carried on in the preaching place has yielded no apparent results. In Kagoshima, the church has had no settled pastor, but has received the services of the Rev.

Mr. Murakata, and has contributed to his support. There has been an increase in the attendance at the services. The church at Karatsu which, as was reported last year, had suffered much from the dishonesty of its former pastor, has succeeded in regaining its title to the church property, nearly lost through his trickery ; and under the care of the Rev. Mr. Tomegawa is recovering its spiritual prosperity as well. In the church at Saga attendance at the services has increased. Three new members were baptized, one a public school teacher who is faithful in the face of opposition ; and there are several candidates for baptism. Work has been carried on in three towns easily accessible by rail. There has been an advance in the direction of self-support.

In the 12 outstations with resident evangelists, work has been carried on regularly, opportunities for seed sowing improved, and a few have been added to the Church. The stations under Mr. Oltman's care have all been visited, some of them several times during the year; but Dr. Stout's time being taken up with school work and Mr. Peeke being absent, little visiting was done in their fields. The work among the Eta in Usabara has been given up, as no visible results came from it ; and the worker, not being qualified for other work, has been dismissed. Four evangelists have resigned nominally for different reasons ; but Dr. Stout's opinion is that inadequate salaries had much to do with their leaving. Four outstations, where work has long been carried on, are left without workers; and contraction, rather than expansion, is the order of the day. This with opportunities for new work waiting on every side; with the new treaties in operation, and the way of access to the people open as never before.

The Christians of the *Chinzei* Presbytery have contributed *yen* 200 more than last year.

Southern Pres.
Mission

The Southern Presbyterian Mission has 10 families and 8 single women who occupy 7 stations.

Japanese
assistants

The Rev. and Mrs. W. C. Buchanan, Miss Houston and Miss Sterling have been absent on furlough during the year. The Rev. and Mrs. S. R. Hope and Miss Evans left Japan on furlough this spring. The Rev. and Mrs. W. B. McIlvaine returned from furlough last fall; and Miss Atkinson, newly appointed, came out and was stationed at Kochi. The Mission sustains one boarding school for girls; and employs 15 evangelists, 3 or 4 of whom are graduates of a mission academy. It has expended yen 3020 for evangelistic work, and yen 929 for educational. With one exception reports from this Mission say that the new treaties have made no change in conditions of evangelistic work. A meeting for workers held twice a year has been fruitful of good and to the spiritual advantage of the workers. At the sessions during the day reports are given, practical problems discussed, Scripture topics studied, and special prayer meetings held. At night, public lectures are delivered all over the neighborhood.

The Kinjo Jo Gakko, at Nagoya, in care of Miss Moore, Kinjo Jo Gakko. has been carried on as usual. The school has an 8 years' course, consisting of the Higher Primary School course and four years beyond. There are now 35 pupils; 2 were graduated at the last commencement. There have been 8 baptisms during the year, and there are 16 Christians in school. The work of the older pupils for children has been interesting and encouraging. The school is 12 years old. Of its 20 graduates, there are 3 in evangelistic work as mission helpers, and 2 are in the Bible school, preparing for Bible work. The expense of the school to the Mission is yen 934.

The Rev. and Mrs. Walter McS. Buchanan in Taka- Evangelistic Work. matsu are the only missionaries in the whole of Sanuki Province. As the town is on the railroad and the country roads are good, they can reach any of their outstations in a day. There has been good progress in the work, with increased attendance at church and Sunday-school. Twelve adults have been baptized, and there are now 14 inquirers. The attitude of the official class toward Christianity is better than last year. In one town, by special invitation, a Bible class has been carried on regularly in the police station; and in Zentsuji, a garrison town, work has been begun by request in the garrison prison, the head man being a Christian; and now nearly all the prison officials are inquirers, and have promised *yen* 5 a month for the evangelist's expenses. Recently, the chief of police in Takamatsu specially requested Mr. Buchanan to teach Christianity to one of the criminals; and it is hoped this will lead to an opening for general work in that prison. The street preaching has proved successful beyond their hopes, good and attentive audiences being the rule. Mr. Buchanan believes this to be the best way of bringing the gospel to the people in the country towns.

Okazaki
The Okazaki station is occupied by the Rev. and Mrs. S. P. Fulton. The Buddhists there continue their opposition, but the Christians are doing what they can for the advance of the gospel and have increased in liberality. The number of inquirers has increased. The Christian women have kept up their weekly meetings, and are earnest in their efforts to bring in the non-Christians. The Sabbath-school has increased in numbers, and there is less opposition from the school teachers. The great drawback to the work has been the lack of workers. During the greater part of the year, there has been only one evangelist connected with the station; it being impossible to fill the vacancy caused by the death of one of the workers last summer. The outstations are within a day's journey, but it requires hard traveling to reach some of them.

Susaki
The Rev. and Mrs. J. B. Moore are alone at Susaki, which is a new field and has not much to report. North, west, and south-west of the town is a mountainous country almost wholly unworked. To eight of the places where work has been begun, it is possible to go by bicycle; but to other places the traveler must walk, and it takes more than a day to reach them. There are as yet no baptized Christians in the field, but there are several candidates for baptism who are zealously working to lead their friends to the light. Mr. Moore is convinced of the importance of personal, private conversation with those who have

become somewhat interested in the truth through the public services.

Tokushima

The Rev. and Mrs. H. W. Myers and Miss Patton report for Tokushima, which is also the station of the Rev. and Mrs. S. R. Hope when they are on the field. The work in the city has made slow progress. There have been a few baptisms, and there are a few inquirers. The station has lost many Christians by removal to other localities, and their places have not been filled by Chriatians coming in. Mr. Myers would urge the importance of the pastor or missionary, from whose care Christians remove, reporting the fact to the church or missionary to whose field they go, as Christians so often will not make themselves known as such in a new place, but if sought out will keep up their duties as Church members. One of the outstations is a long hard day's journey distant; the others are nearer. At one of these, there was great interest for a while; hundreds attended every service, many homes were thrown open for preaching services, and many were studying the Bible. Of these, three were baptized and a few continue as inquirers.

Kochi

The Rev. and Mrs. R. E. McIlvaine and Miss Atkinson are at Kochi. Miss Evans also was there most of the year. I quote verbatim from Mr. McIlvaine's report: "We are trying to put in practice the method recommended by the Council in 1897; viz., to employ fewer workers, and to get the private Christians to meet together for prayer and Bible study. We have now in our field six groups of Christians who have services regularly every Sabbath, being visited by the missionary or his helper, or both, about once a month. One of these groups has kept up this practice for a number of years, having never had a paid evangelist. Some of our best and staunchest Christians were from this place. The church in Kochi is of course self-supporting and self-governing. Two other groups, Akai and Gomen, are entirely self-supporting, but have not been organized into churches yet. The latter have been without a pastor since last October, but hope to get a preacher as soon as they can find a suitable man. The Motoyama group pays half the salary of their preacher; the other half is paid by the Mission. This is the only place where there is a stationed preacher who receives help from the Mission. The Christians at all the outstations pay all rents and incidental expenses." Five of the outstations are a day's journey from Kochi; some of the towns where there are inquirers to be visited are over two days' journey distant. Mrs. McIlvaine has had children's meetings in an Eta village and Miss Atkinson in Kochi, but most of her time was spent upon the language. Miss Evans, up to the time of her departure, kept up a number of meetings for women and children.

The Rev. and Mrs. H. B. Price and Miss Dowd are at Kobe. The church there has made decided gains in membership and liberality, and has voted that from July it will assume the entire support of the pastor. It has been receiving help from the Board of Home Missions of the Japanese Church for the past two years. Mr. Price's work is all in Kobe. The new regulations there have tended to the hindrance of new work. Street preaching has become more difficult, and there has been great delay in getting permission to open new chapels. Mr. Price fears that where there is local prejudice in new fields the present regulations may prevent the opening of new preaching places. But the greatest hindrance to all the progress of the work in Kobe has been the lack of evangelists and Bible women. The work could be greatly increased, if only there were more workers. Also, there is great need of local centres for the distribution of Christian literature. Good books require good colporteurs to bring them to the notice of the Christians and the public. Mr. Price also advocates, coöperation of the Missions of the Council in connection with the employing and locating of evangelists, and the locating and moving of missionaries. He thinks a quick-moving, light brigade of missionaries who would stay only two or three years in a place, might greatly help the work in the smaller cities; and that an aversion to moving on the part of the missionaries is seemingly a disadvantage to the working of the whole field.

Mrs. Price has carried on a cooking class, with a Bible lesson following, twice a week. The women are getting interested in the Bible, and the class is hopeful. She has also three children's classes, and greatly needs the help of a Bible woman to follow up the lessons with house to house visiting. Miss Dowd's work has been among the Christian women in Kobe and Hyōgo. She labors especially among those who have become indifferent; holding two weekly Bible classes and making many calls on them in their homes.

In Nagoya, the Rev. and Mrs. R. E. McAlpine, the Nagoya Rev. and Mrs. C. K. Cumming and Miss Wimbish are in charge of the evangelistic work. The church, which has been independent for several years, has had a year of good progress and success. The mission preaching place, which it is hoped is the necleus of a new church, has not prospered so well, for last summer the evangelist in charge was found to be mixing up his Christianity with Shintoism; and when he was dismissed, he drew away a number of the young men with him. As yet, no suitable man has been found to take his place, so there is no mission evangelist in the city. The country work has been more encouraging. Mr. MacAlpine has a number of places to be visited, but by bicycle he can reach any one of them in a day. The only new method used has been the selling of Scripture portions, which has proved to be a very satisfactory and enjoyable work. He has baptized 8 adults. Of Mr. Cumming's outstations, four or five are a day's journey away. There have been 5 baptisms in this district. Work among the women has suffered greatly for lack of workers.

The Cumberland Presbyterian Mission is composed of 5 Cumberland Pres. Mission families and 7 single women, and occupies 5 stations in Osaka and the provinces of Izumi, Kii, and Wakayama. The Rev. and Mrs. G. W. Van Horne have been absent all the year, and Miss Freeland has left for furlough during the year. Miss Gardner has returned from furlough, and is located at Shingu, Kii province; and the Rev. and Mrs.

35

J. C. Worley, newly appointed, are stationed at Tsu, Ise. Mrs. Lyon has been transferred from Tsu to Osaka.

Japanese assistants During the year, the Mission employed 3 lay workers and 11 pastors and evangelists; 4 of whom were graduates of the academic department of a mission school. Recently, however, two of these, ordained men, have withdrawn from the work, one to go to America and one on account of throat trouble. The Mission expends about *yen* 2000 for evangelistic work, and *yen* 1200 for educational work.

Wilmina Jo Gakko The Wilmina Jo Gakko is now in charge of Miss Morgan. She writes that it is difficult to report for the school, as it was closed from July till January. However, it is now in a promising condition, with good prospects for the future. There were 32 pupils in school at the end of April. None were graduated last year. The Christian spirit is evident in the work of all the teachers, and all in school feel it and are influenced by it. Sixteen of the pupils are Christians. Three of the former graduates are teaching in mission schools. The school costs the Mission *yen* 1300.

Bible training School at Tsu The Bible Training School at Tsu is a family school; the pupils living in Mrs. Drennan's house. No pupils are admitted, save those who really want to fit themselves to be Bible women. Graduates from the Higher Primary Schools can enter the Bible course. There were 13 pupils in school during the year; one graduated, and there are now 8 in the Bible course. There have been 5 baptisms during the year. Of the nine graduates, 3 are teaching in mission schools, and the other 6 are Bible women. The school receives no mission funds, as societies at home support individual pupils. About *yen* 75 a year per pupil pays for board, books, and all the school expenses. The Rev. and Mrs. J. C. Worley, in addition to their study of the language, are now helping Mrs. Drennan in the school, thus giving her more time for the evangelistic work which she does with her Bible women. Her workers have distributed tracts in every village and hamlet in Iga Province and many in Ise. Meetings for women and children are held regularly in many places. The church at Tsu has grown, not only in numbers, but in spirituality and in zeal, and hopes soon to attain to self-support. The Sunday-school uses the International Lessons, and has written examinations quarterly. Pupils number 50; and 29 adults have been baptized there, and 7 at Ueno, in Iga. In the different towns there are many inquirers. Mrs. Lyon while in Tsu taught English in the Bible school and had an afternoon English school for boys and young men.

The Rev. and Mrs. J. B. Hail are stationed in Waka- yama. Besides the church, there are two preaching places in the city. The church, in addition to the usual services and a weekly woman's meeting, has an early morning prayer meeting monthly, and a weekly work meeting. This latter begun to raise money to pay off the church debt, was continued because of its social benefit and to raise money for a new church in the future. All these meetings are well attended; and, since last fall, the church has been self-supporting taking, however, only half of the pastor's time. One of the preaching places was in charge of Mrs. Hail, and the other in charge of Miss Morgan up to January when the latter was transferred to the school in Osaka. She especially tried to reach those who were outside the influence of the church, and had a number of Bible classes, weekly meetings, and Sunday-schools. She had large and interesting class of girls, employed in a thread winding establishment. The proprietor of the house invited her to come, and he and his wife attended the meetings and were much pleased with the effect of the teaching upon the character and conduct of the girls. The older girls of well-to-do families were difficult to reach, and Miss Morgan thinks the mission schools are needed to get hold of the girls of the higher classes.

The church at Tanabe has been self-supporting since last July, in the same way as that at Wakayama, by taking only half of the pastor's time, and has had an unusually prosperous year. Miss Leavitt is stationed there. Her work is connected with the church and confined to the town. She has two women's meetings weekly,

37

average attendance 15; and a weekly Bible class composed of the wives of the Middle School teachers. A knitting class, which is preceded by a half hour of religious instruction, has grown from 12 members to 50, since a charge 3 *sen* a month was made for tuition. The money from this goes to the church Sunday-school. The Sunday-school is graded and uses the International Lessons. There are 70 pupils.

Mr. Hail speaks of Shingu, where Miss Gardner is stationed as having had a prosperous year. He mentions 18 other places where there are Christians or inquirers whom he has regularly visited. He has made 935 calls and visits, and held religious conversation with 1218 persons.

Dr. and Mrs. A. D. Hail and the Rev. and Mr. G. G. Hudson are in Osaka. Dr. Hail finds conditions under the new treaties more favorable as concerns the renting of chapels, abolition of passports, and the general acceptance of the foreign missionary as a part of the new order of things. Four of his outstations are a day's journey away and six are nearer. Mr. Hudson's work is all near the city. During the year, he has published "A History of the Early Church as Found in the New Testament." Miss Alexander is stationed at Takatsuki, in Setsu, but no report has been received from there. In the whole field

of the Mission there have been 63 baptisms during the year.

The West Japan Presbyterian Mission has 11 families and 9 single women, and occupies 6 stations.

The Rev. and Mrs. A. V. Bryan have been absent all the year. During the year, Miss Palmer, the Rev. and Mrs. J. B. Porter, and Miss Porter went to America on furlough, while the Rev. and Mrs. J. W. Doughty, and the Rev. and Mrs. G. W. Fulton, have returned from furlough. Miss M. Nivling, newly appointed, arrived last fall, and is stationed at Osaka. The Rev. and Mrs. H. Brokaw have been transferred from Kanazawa to Hiroshima; the Rev. and Mrs. G. W. Fulton from Fukui to Kanazawa; Miss Settlemyer from Osaka to Kyoto; and Miss Glenn from Osaka to Kanazawa. The Mission carries on four kindergartens, two primary schools, and three higher schools for girls. It employs 25 pastors and evangelists, of whom 14 are graduates of mission academies; and about 45 teachers in the schools, many of whom give only part time. It has expended *yen* 9482 for evangelistic work, and *yen* 6457 for educational work.

Hokuriku Jo Gakko Kanazawa

The Kanazawa Hokuriku Jo Gakko has been in charge of Miss Shaw and Miss Glenn. The grade of the school corresponds roughly to that of the Higher Primary Schools and four years beyond, with a corresponding course in English. There have been 50 pupils in school during the year. Five graduated at the last commencement; and there were 37 in attendance at the end of April. There have been no baptisms during the year, but nine girls have been converted, though their parents will not allow them to receive baptism. Counting these, there are 22 Christians in school. The spiritual life of the school is at high tide. The Christian Endeavor Society has 30 active members, and its weekly meetings are attended by all in the school. The visit of Dr. Clark, in February, was a great stimulus and inspiration. The pupils formerly attended the church Sunday-school, but this year a special Sunday-school has been carried on in the school. The school is 14 years old. Of the 48 graduates, 5 are teaching in mission schools, and 5 are in evangelistic work. The expense of the school to the Mission was *yen* 1259.

Kojo Jo Gakko Yamaguchi

In Yamaguchi, Miss Bigelow is in charge of the Kojo Jo Gakko, and the new treaties have made it possible for her to become the principal. In addition to this, she and Miss Palmer have received license from the Department of Education to teach in the vernacular. The school has an English and a Japanese course, the grade corresponding in general to the government Higher Primary Schools and three years beyond. There is also a kindergarten connected with it. There were 31 pupils attending regularly during the year. Two were graduated at the commencement, and there were 28 in school at the end of April. The conservative prejudice against girls' education in Yamaguchi is being overcome; and this year for the first time the number of day pupils has exceeded the number of boarders. There are 13 Christians in the school, 2 not yet baptized. The school is 10 years old. Of its 14 graduates, 6 are teaching in mission schools, and one is in evangelistic work. The cost of the school to Mission was *yen* 1509.

Naniwa Jo Gakko

The Naniwa Jo Gakko in Osaka is in charge of Miss Garvin and Miss Nivling. During the year, the school has dropped the Industrial Department and the lowest year of the regular course, which has reduced the number of pupils; but the school is in good working order, and the number of boarding pupils has doubled. There have been 77 in attendance during the year, and there are now 48. Four were graduated at the last commencement. The local government has granted more privileges this year than ever before. There are 18 Christians in the school, and 4 are desiring baptism. The daily Bible classes continue to be a prominent feature of the school. About a third of the pupils attend the Sunday services and the weekly prayer meeting. Three of the graduates are teaching in mission schools, and two are in evangelistic work The cost of the school to the Mission is *yen* 2597.

Eiwa Sho Gakko

Of the primary day schools, the Eiwa Sho Gakko in Kanazawa was in charge of Miss Porter and Miss Luther. The school has a common and a higher course, and there is a kindergarten connected with it. Last fall the school withdrew from government control and is now a distinctly Christian school, with its object stated in the catalogue. Only two pupils were lost by this change. The examination at the close of the year by the local officials in the lowest department was successfully passed, and teachers sent by the government pronounced the work well done. There are now 53 pupils in school, and 20 in the kindergarten. The school costs the Mission *yen* 625.

Primary School

The two primary schools in Osaka in charge of Miss Haworth have during the year been united into one, the Kiiku Sho Gakko, to save teaching force. The work of the school is very encouraging. There are 157 pupils in attendance. The tuitions cover rent and incidental ex-

40

penses. Daily Christian instruction is given. Eight of the pupils attend the Sunday-school held in the building. The 5 teachers are all Christians and two of the pupils. The school costs the Mission less than *yen* 40. Miss Haworth has also charge of a night school for young men. Eighteen attend, all of whom are unbelievers; Christians who apply being directed to study elsewhere. The school is held in the preaching place, and the students usually stay for the Sunday and Wednesday evening services. On three evenings special Bible study is given. She also has a semi-weekly Bible class for women attended by school teachers. Night school

The two kindergartens in Kyoto are in charge of Miss Kelly. The number of the pupils is 81. There are two Bible women who give their time to visiting in the homes of the pupils. Miss Kelly is more and more persuaded of the usefulness of kindergartens as evangelistic agencies. The greatest difficulty is to get the proper trained helpers, and she wishes to impress upon the Council the importance of sustaining well our higher schools, as trained women are needed for the work. Miss Kelly has also a number of English classes which she believes to be a very successful branch of work, and hopes to continue. She says, "The daily demand of personal inquirers has increased, as have opportunities in every line. Some of the most conservative classes of Kyoto are accessible; and while there has been much seed-sowing, there has been harvesting also." Kindergartens English classes

The church work in Kyoto has gone on steadily, the members showing a good and earnest spirit. The women's meetings are kept up, largely by the efforts of a few of the church women. Dr. Alexander and Miss Settlemeyer are in charge of the evangelistic work in Kyoto, but no report has been received from either of them. Church work

The Kanazawa station occupied by the Rev. and Mrs. J. G. Dunlop and the Rev. and Mrs. G. W. Fulton, has two outstations with resident evangelists. Most of the work in the city is in connection with the church which, though independent, offers many opportunities to the Kanazawa missionary to give needed and effective help; and through the church many unbelievers are reached. Mr. Dunlop believes the missionaries can not do better than to give much of their strength to working with the church, as in this way they can do much towards making these early churches models for those who come after, and save them possibly from error both in doctrine and practice. In the country work, but little progress can be reported; the very strong anti-Christian prejudice making in difficult to rent places for occasional meetings and audiences are small. The new treaties have had a somewhat liberalizing effect upon the people, and more doors are now open than before. Selling the Scriptures in the street and from door to door has been successfully done, and this has also given opportunities to preach the gospel to the groups which gather round.

Fukui

The work at Fukui, an old stronghold of Buddhism and conservatism, is in charge of the Rev. and Mrs. W. Y. Jones. The field has over a quarter of a million of inhabitants; and they are the only foreigners in the place. There is only one outstation with a resident evangelist, but regular weekly work has been carried on in three other towns accessible by rail; and much occasional work has been done in neighboring towns and villages. In some places, strong opposition was met with, but in many places the audiences were large. Mr. Jones publishes a semimonthly paper, Light in Darkness, a simple exposition of Scripture passages intended for inquirers. This is sent to all who ask for it and has now a circulation of 450. Tracts have been faithfully distributed at the houses in Fukui and the neighboring towns. Of these tracts, Ando's Experience in Hawaii, Dr. Verbeck's Answers to Objections, and Dr. Gordon's On Buddhism have attracted the most attention and comment. A great many copies of the gospels have been sold in this same way, going from house to house. In regard to this, Mrs. Jones says, "As we go about in this way, the people see we are in earnest and really believe our religion, and are interested in them and their spiritual welfare; so an interest is created and openings for regular work secured. I think we can accomplish much more in this way than if we spent the same amount of time and strength in teaching English. Did we fill up our time with English classes and confine our work to our residence town, in all probability, these people whom we are now reaching, would never have an opportunity to hear of Christianity and what it teaches." Though last fall the people were absorbed in getting their homes restored after the great flood, and an earthquake and a fire have further devasted the neighborhood, Mrs. Jones has been able to carry on 10 weekly meetings regularly the latter part of the year.

The Osaka station has been manned by the Rev. and Osaka Mrs. T. C. Winn and the Rev. and Mr. Mrs. B. C. Haworth. Of the two self-supporting churches there, one has made progress, while the other has merely held its own. Mr. Winn reports fair progress made for some of the work under his charge, and no progress whatever in others. Conditions under the new treaties are a little more favorable. His outstations are near Osaka. Mr. Haworth's five outstations are all more than a day's journey away. In one place the work, formerly promising, has been nearly destroyed by Dowiism. The evangelist, who has a brother with Dowie, has accepted that faith. In the province of Iyo, there is promise of an abundant harvest, if only a sufficient force of workers can be obtained. Financial difficulties have compelled more than half of the workers to give up the ministry. Mr. Haworth considers the supply of evangelists to be one of the most pressing questions of the day, and hopes that the Council will take the matter into consideration.

The Rev. and Mr. F. S. Curtis and the Rev. and Mrs. Yamaguchi J. B. Ayres are at Yamaguchi. Of their 12 outstations, 8 are a day's journey away. The general attitude of the people is more favorable to Christianity. There have been 20 baptisms during the year and an advance towards self-support. The church at Wakamatsu has become entirely self-supporting; and with the help of the pastor of this church, two other bodies of believers have united

43

and become independent of mission funds. The station has emphasized village, wayside and personal work, and work among the students. Mrs. Curtis has published a little booklet, Talks for Mothers.

The field of the Rev. and Mr. J. W. Doughty and the Rev. and Mrs. H. Brokaw extends for 50 miles east and 30 miles west of Hiroshima. The church at Hiroshima is independent, and the missionaries have no direct relations with it; though they are on the best of terms and give assistance with the music, occasional preaching and advice, when requested. There are three outstations with resident evangelists. These are within a day's journey, though the best part of two days must be spent in order to hold a service in any one of them. The general work of the station is of the usual kind ; preaching, Sunday-school work, and tract distribution. A monthly paper is published for distribution among non-believers.

The East Japan Presbyterian Mission comprises 7 families and 9 single women. Of these, Dr. and Mrs. McCartee and Mrs. John Ballagh are absent. Last fall, Miss Youngman, and this summer, the Rev. and Mrs. T. M. MacNair returned from furlough. Dr. Alexander also returned and went to Kyoto in the West Japan Mission. Of the 20 members now on the field, 15 are in Tokyo, 1 in Yokohama, and 4 in the Hokkaido. The Mission sustains one Bible Womans Training School, two boarding schools for girls, two primary schools, a day school for girls, an industrial school for girls; and, in connection with the North Japan Mission of the Reformed (Dutch) Church, carries on the Academic and Theological Departments of the Meiji Gakuin. The Mission has evangelistic work in Tokyo and the vicinity, extending to Utsunomiya and Kujukuri ; in 3 places in Niigata Ken; and in 5 places in the Hokkaido. It employs 23 pastors and evangelists, one of whom is a graduate of a mission academy, and 11 or 12 Bible women ; and in the schools about 50 teachers, many of whom give only a part of their time. The Mission has expended for evangelistic work *yen* 7377, and for educational work *yen* 9922.

44

Dr. Wyckoff, of the Reformed (Dutch) Mission, reports for the Meiji Gakuin Academic Department. " Last year when the school closed for the summer, there were 130 pupils in attendance with every prospect of an increase in the fall. Then came the " Instruction " of the Minister of Education ; and in order that it might continue religious instruction, the school gave up its connection with the government. Because of this, a number of students left ; so that during the winter there were only 90 in attendance. Six pupils were graduated in April, and the new year began with 80 pupils, but some have entered since. Though the schools would seem to have received a great blow from the " Instruction," yet some are beginning to think it a blessing in disguise by its attracting attention to Christianity, and by making Christians and Christian institutions more vertebrate and less disposed to consult expediency by trying to conform themselves to their non-Christian surroundings. The school work has gone on steadily and satisfactorily, and Bible classes and religious meetings have been kept up as in former years." There have been four baptisms since the last Council report (but after the statistical report ending April 30 was given), and there are 21 Christians now in school. The school is 24 years old. Of the 134 graduates, 6 are at present teaching in mission schools, and 5 are in evangelistic work in the employ of missions. Fifteen others are in pastoral and evangelistic work, not aided by mission funds. The expense of the school to the Missions is *yen* 4200 annually. The Rev. Mr. H. M. Landis is the member of the Presbyterian Mission connected with the school. In addition to his work there, he has taught a class in the Shiba Sunday-school; and several of his pupils have united with that church during the year. He has also done Bible teaching and occasional preaching in other places, and as a member of the Sunday-school Literature Committee has spent much time in the preparation of the monthly Sunday-school Teachers Journal.

The Theological Department of the Meiji Gakuin as well as the Academic Department has a Japanese Principal, the Rev. K. Ibuka. Dr. Imbrie is at present the only missionary teaching in the school, and gives five hours a week to class-room work. Two students were graduated at the last commencement. At present, there are only 5 in the school, all in the first or Junior year of the course. Only one of these is a graduate of an academic department. All of the students do evangelistic work in addition to their studies. The cost of the department is *yen* 2540. In addition to his work in the Theological Department, Dr. Imbrie contributes regularly to the Fukuin Shimpo, and occasionly to the Biblical Expositor, and has had the general care of a part of the work in Tokyo and in Niigata Ken, but says there is nothing of special interest to report concerning its condition or progress.

Seisho Gakuin

During Mrs. MacNair's absence Miss West has had the entire charge of the Bible Training School in Tokyo. There have been 17 pupils in the school during the year. Two were graduated, and there are 13 now in the school. The number of pupils is less than in previous years, but the school is in good condition. Two of the Bible women, doing outside work, now live in the school and their reports of opportunities to work have been a stimulus to the pupils. Of the 50 graduates of the school, 20 are in Bible work in the employ of Missions; 16 have married pastors or evangelists, and three are employed in mission schools. The schools costs the Mission *yen* 1142, but this includes the support of the women while in school and while in vacation work in the country. Miss West has the direction of several Bible women who work in Tokyo and in four outstations. The Sunday-schools where they teach have improved greatly. The children prepare lessons at home, and contribute money for benevolent purposes. In two places the Bible women have taught some of the Christians to play the organ, so that their churches may have organists.

Joshi Gakuin

The Joshi Gakuin, the school for girls in Tokyo, has had an exceptionally prosperous year. Miss Milliken, Miss Gardner and Miss Ballagh are the missionaries in the school, and are assisted by the Misses Ruth and Grace

46

Thompson as regular teachers. The institution has the strongest corps of Japanese teachers it has ever had. The course of the school is ten years long, and in general covers that of the Higher Primary Schools and six years beyond it, with special attention given to English. One hundred and fifty pupils have been in attendance throughout the year; 7 were graduated in the spring, and a number of new pupils entered. The attendance at the end of April was 180, of whom 93 were boarders. There have been 3 baptisms during the year, and the number of Christians in the school is 65. The value of the daily Bible study is emphasized; to it all other classroom work tends, and for it prepares. Of the 48 graduates of the school (since 1890), 19 are at present teaching in mission schools, 5 are in evangelistic work in the employ of Missions, and 2 are trained Christian nurses. The remaining 22 have married. The cost of the school to the Mission is *yen* 2826. Miss Milliken, besides her work in the school, has the direction of two Bible women; and, as also the other two ladies, has Sunday-school work and Bible classes and other work in connection with the churches and elsewhere. Miss Gardner has daily Bible classes for outsiders in her home. Miss Ballagh has charge of two schools or daily classes for poor children; one in Tsunohazu and one in Yokohama.

The Hokkusei Jo Gakko in Sapporo is in charge of Miss Smith. The course of study corresponds to that of the Higher Primary Schools and three years beyond. There have been 48 pupils in regular attendance, and a large number in irregular attendance during the year. The present number of pupils is 68, only 6 of whom are supported. One was graduated last commencement. There have been 5 baptisms since last May, and 21 of the pupils are Christians. A Sunday-school of street children numbering 70 is taught by the older Christian girls. The school is 12 years old. Of the 18 graduates, 3 are engaged in teaching in mission schools. The cost of the school to the Mission was *yen* 1640.

The Seishu Jo Gakko in Otaru is a Higher Primary day school for girls in charge of Miss Rose. It was begun

Hokkusei Jo Gakko

Seishu Jo Gakko

47

five years ago, and has two kindergartens connected with it. In all there are now 90 pupils in attendance. The school has prospered during the year. Last fall some of the pupils had to be dismissed on account of the government regulations, but opposition was a tonic. The first class will be graduated next April. As the school is helped by private funds, the Mission pays only *yen* 120 to its support. Miss Rose has 6 Sunday-schools in connection with her work. In these, 5 girls, two of them graduates of an older mission school, are doing good work as her assistants.

Primary schools in Tokyo

The two Primary Schools, Keimo No. 1 and No. 2, under the care of Mrs. McCauley, suffered much from the new educational regulations. About 200 pupils were obliged to leave, and the schools opened in October with less than 50 in attendance. The number has now grown to 130. The pupils have a daily Bible lesson for 45 minutes, and all attend the Sunday-school. During the year, all of the homes of the pupils have been visited, some of them many times, by the Christian teachers. The schools receive *yen* 600 from the Mission in addition to the rent. Mrs. McCauley also visits weekly at the Charity Hospital where gospel teaching is gladly received.

Shinagawa Primary School

Last fall, because of the new regulations, Miss West thought it best to close the Shinagawa Primary School, rather than to continue it as a purely charity school. The building is now used as a preaching place. Many of the former pupils come regularly to the Sunday-school, and bring their friends from the public schools with them. A weekly knitting class and Bible meeting is also held in the building. In April the kindergarten was re-opened as a distinctly Christian school, and has now 40 children. Total expense *yen* 200.

Yokohama Primary School

The Primary School in Yokohama, under the care of Miss Case, was also closed last fall. An industrial school has been opened in its place. Sewing, embroidery, etc., with English and Japanese branches, are taught; and the pastor of Shiloh church gives a half hour of Bible instruction daily. Miss Case has the oversight of the work of two Bible women, and has Bible class and Sunday-school work.

No detailed report has been received of the general Evangelistic Work evangelistic work in and around Tokyo. There are 12 or 15 places where work is carried on. Mr. MacNair has been absent on furlough during the year, and Dr. Thompson has been the only member of the Mission giving his whole time to the work. He says, "It is distinctly depressing to find many of our best trained evangelists leaving their fields of labor for other occupations; one of our men has gone to Chicago and joined Dowie's work there." Concerning self-support, he says, "It looks as if an effort were being made to solve the question by getting rid of everything that requires support rather than supporting it." Dr. Thompson has also prepared and published a catechism on the Confession of Faith of the Church of Christ in Japan.

Miss Youngman reports concerning the Ueno and Ueno and Kamejima Missions Kamejima Missions. The daily and nightly preaching services have been continued in these places throughout the year, as also the Sunday open-air service in the park. At each meeting, there are two speakers; and tracts are distributed. About 35000 people attended these services during the year. From time to time applicants for admission to the various churches have said that they first heard the truth there. The Buddhists applied for permission to have similar services in the park, and at first it seemed as if the same locality would be assigned to them; but, in response to a request, a place was given them elsewhere. The Ueno Mission has completed its tenth year. For some years, work similar to this was carried on in a tent at Kamakura, and thousands were reached by it, but "lack of funds has shut our tent away in a box, and we have only one Bible woman who works there as she can, with an occasional visit from an evangelist from Tokyo."

From the Hokkaido station, Mr. Pierson reports. All Hokkaido that has been written of the urgency of continued and earnest effort on behalf of this island, should have a new line underscored. There has been progress all along the line in the increased opportunities caused by new land

49

being opened, new facilities for travel, new people coming in, and the abandoning of old tried-and-found-wanting religions. There has been progress in the wider diffusion of gospel truth through preaching and Bible and tract distribution, in the growing sense of shame over the social evil and attempts to combat it, and in the growing recognition that civilization without Christianity is not true civilization." Three of the churches are self-supporting, and have made good progress in faith and numbers. The five places under the care of the Mission are all progressing and promising, and have increased in numbers. Otaru has built a pastor's house, and is looking forward to self-support. In Mombetsu, the Christians have taken the lead in a determined, and apparently successful, agitation to prevent the establishment of places of iniquity in the town. In Mororan, Takegawa and Kamikawa, the growth has been not only in numbers, but in moral tone and a widening of lines of work. Mr. and Mrs. Pierson are now in Sapporo, but hope to move to Kamikawa. One of the outstations is now more than a day's journey away, and five can each be reached in a day. He adds, "What impresses me most is the transcendent importance of getting every individual of our generation into intelligent contact with the way of salvation. The Japanese heart is lonely. There is a religious vacuum. We can ask no better demand for what we have to give them than there is at present. We are not keeping up with one-tenth of our opportunities. We need one new missionary family, two new missionary women, four evangelists, and some Bible women."

Mission of the U. P. Church of Scotland — The Mission of the United Presbyterian Church of Scotland has only two families, both resident in Tokyo. Their work is so blended with the work of other Missions in Tokyo that it is hard to draw the line between. Mr. Waddell preaches all over Tokyo in the churches of other Missions, and helps all ; but is especially interested in the Ueno Mission, which has been reported above. He found more interested listeners there this year than ever before, and the audiences have been exceptionally respectful and courteous. He thinks the Buddhist preaching in the park is an advantage to the Christian work; as they, having no glad news for the people, are not able to hold their attentions; and thus a fine opportunity is given for comparing the two religions. There need be no fear for the future for the cause of Christ in Japan, if only the gospel is preached to the people. Mr. Waddell would urge the Council to urge their home Boards to send out more men.

Mr. Davidson's principal work during the year has been the preparation and distribution in certain districts in Tokyo of a progressive series of tracts teaching the fundamental truths regarding salvation.

The North Japan Mission of the Reformed (Dutch) Church comprises 6 families and 6 single women, and it occupies 6 stations. Miss Winn has been absent during the year; and in March Miss Thompson went home on furlough. Miss Moulton returned from furlough in September. In the fall, the Rev. and Mrs. H. Harris removed from Ichinoseki to Aomori, and Miss Wyckoff removed from Ferris Seminary to Ueda, where she spent the winter studying the language, returning to Ferris Seminary in the spring to take Miss Thompson's place. In addition to its part in the Meiji Gakuin, the Mission carries on one Higher School for girls. It employs 16 evangelists, none of whom are graduates of a mission academy, but 5 have studied for a longer or shorter time in such an academy. The Mission has expended yen 5648 for evangelistic, and yen 8405 for educational work. Dr. Wyckoff's report for the Meiji Gakuin has already been given. In addition to his work in the school, he has preached in Japanese and given magic lantern exhibitions of Bible scenes.

North Japan Mission of the R. C. A. (Dutch)

Ferris Seminary, the Higher School for girls in Yokohama, is in charge of the Rev. and Mrs. E. S. Booth, assisted by Miss Moulton and Miss Wyckoff. The school has enjoyed a condition of healthfulness during the year, but not one of special growth. The passing under the

Ferris Seminary

local educational supervision in October was accomplished without difficulty, and practically no change is apparent. Three pupils were graduated at the last commencement, and there are 54 in attendance. The grade of the school corresponds to that of the Higher Primary Schools and 4 years beyond. The Bible course has been in operation during the year; and Mr. Booth has given much time to preparation for the lessons and to classroom work there and in the Grammar Department. Mrs. Booth has been compelled by necessity to devote her time to the instruction of her own children. Miss Thompson had the chief English teaching until her return to America. Miss Moulton, besides the larger part of the musical instruction has done much Bible and English teaching. It is Mr. Booth's opinion that the agitation on the part of some Missions against the so-called (but wrongly so-called) higher education in mission schools, and the consequent cutting down of the grade, is chiefly responsible for the lack of numbers; and he would suggest that the wisest policy would be to return to the higher standard. There have been 4 baptisms during the year, and there are 24 Christians in the school. The school is 25 years old. Of the 72 graduates, 8 are teaching in mission schools, and 8 are in evangelistic work in the employ of Missions. Another former pupil, not a graduate, is working with the Salvation Army. The cost of the school to the Mission is *yen* 5050. Since January, Mr. Booth has been acting as pastor of the Union Church of the foreign community in Yokohama.

Evangelistic work The evangelistic work of the Mission is in Aomori, Iwate, Aichi, Shizuoka, Saitama and Shinano Provinces. With the exception of the first two provinces, the work has been been chiefly under the care of the Rev. J. H. Ballagh of Yokohama and he still has the oversight of 10 outstations which are from half a day to four days distant from his residence. There is a resident evangelist in each place. Mr. Ballagh reports 18 baptisms and an increased interest in the hearing of the gospel. He wishes however to emphasize his growing conviction of the importance of the personal presence of a missionary in all central stations, or wherever effective work is contemplated. In regard to self-support, he says, " Little advance has been made, if indeed retrogression has not taken place. The rule that chapel rents and local expenses should be met by the believers and evangelists was complied with on condition that the evangelists' salaries should be raised yen 8 per month, and has not resulted in larger efforts on the part of believers. In three cases, chapels have been built or bought by the Mission, thus doing away with rent."

The Rev. and Mrs. E. Rothesay Miller have been stationed for many years at Morioka, and had charge of the work in the north. Ichinoseki is the only outstation with a resident evangelist. In Morioka, there has been a working evangelist besides the pastor, as the latter gives a large portion of his time to assisting Mrs. Miller in the preparation of Glad Tidings and Little Tidings. There have been a few baptisms in Ichinoseki and 13 in Morioka. The new church building is well located for lecture meetings, and a number of Christian lectures have been given there to large audiences. A meeting for evangelists was held in December attended by all the workers in the north. Pastoral work was the subject that aroused the most interest and discussion. Mr. Miller has also visited all the stations in the Shinano field with great profit, both to the work and himself, in his clearer knowledge thus obtained of the condition of the work there.

Since last September, the Rev. and Mrs. H. Harris have been in Aomori looking after the work during Miss Winn's absence. A very satisfactory church building was completed there last summer. The Christians raised yen 50 for furnishing it. The Sunday services and women's meetings are well attended, but the prayer meetings are not sustained, nor the Sabbath kept as it should be. But few of the church members are really alive to their duties and privileges. There is need of workers who are quick to note needs and opportunities, and to correct wrong views in the church, and stimulate it to activity. Both Mr. and Mrs. Harris, with their two helpers, do much house to house visiting. The Sunday-schools and regular women's meetings and Bible classes are carried on. There are large opportunities for more work.

Nagano

Nagano station is occupied by the Rev. and Mrs. F. S. Scudder and Mrs. Schenck. There is much opposition to Christianity in this old Buddhist stronghold. The temple of Zenkoji held a fifty days' festival this spring, and during that time the city was thronged with pilgrims. The church, which has a membership of 40, has advanced during the year. About two-thirds of the members attend church faithfully; and the prayer meetings are well kept up. The Christians have increased their contributions, and pay *yen* 5 more than last year. They have themselves organized and graded the Sunday-school. The introduction of chain cards by Mrs. Schenck has added to the interest. The increase of inquirers is one of the hopeful signs. People come from unexpected quarters to ask about Christianity. At Nakano, several theatre meetings were held with an average attendance of 1000 people. At first, they were antagonistic, but this decreased at each successive meeting. If the station were supplied with several workers, it seems as though a good harvest might be reaped. Mrs. Schenck with her two helpers has carried on a number of weekly meetings for women and children in Nagano and the vicinity. In some places the opposition of the Buddhists has been open and severe; but on the whole the attendance has been good, and there are more opportunities than she can avail herself of. She has also taught two English Bible classes of young men. Mr. Scudder has also prepared the weekly Leaflets published by the Committee on Sunday-school Literature.

Ueda

In Ueda, the church is independent and self-supporting. Miss Deyo's efforts have been entirely given to ward and village work. Instead of helping the church, it seemed to be more profitable all around to get the church to help her. During previous years, work had been carried on in 8 districts of the city and 15 villages. All the seed-sowing must ultimately tend to the upbuilding of the Ueda church; and when a year ago, her salaried helpers were obliged to leave, an appeal was made to the church

54

to carry on the work. A few volunteers came forward; and since July, no mission funds have been used for salaries. Gradually the number of workers increased, until now 10 weekly neighborhood meetings, in addition to the regular church meetings, are carried on by the Christians. And a number of special lecture meetings have been given in these localities by the pastor and more prominent men in the church. Up to the end of June, all expenses—rent Sunday-school papers, cards, tracts etc.—have been borne by the Mission; but next year the church will assume the rents, and has promised to continue all the old meetings, and is talking of opening new ones. A really earnest, zealous spirit of evangelization is growing in the church. The services are well attended. There have been 8 baptisms and there is quite a large inquirers' class. Funds for needed church improvements and supplies are easily raised, and a group of seven young men can always be called upon to aid in any duty connected with the church. They give out tracts, and sell Bibles giving the 25 per cent commission to the church work. One young man and two women are learning to play the organ that the church may always have an organist. The Mission has turned over all its work in that immediate vicinity to the care of the church, and from last month has no longer any connection with it.

The Womans Union Mission has at present only two members on the field. Last November, Mrs. Pierson, for 28 years a faithful missionary, passed to her home in Heaven; and in January, Miss Dorsey returned to America. The Union Bible School is now in charge of Miss Pratt. At present there are 67 pupils, all of whom are engaged more or less in outside evangelistic work. The girls school is now temporarily in charge of Miss Crosby, who reports 76 pupils in attendance. Connected with the schools, are 7 outside Sunday-schools with 240 pupils.

In regard to the work in Omata, where she had been stationed for some time, Miss Crosby writes, "There is much to encourage in the work here. About 70 now attend the Sunday services. There have been 8 baptisms during the winter and there are a goodly number of inquirers. The present evangelist is not a book-worm, but a bright active man, who goes about among the people continually; and nearly every day persons come to his room in the chapel to inquire about Christianity and its doctrines." Miss Crosby's two helpers are constantly working there, and she herself is only temporarily absent.

German Reformed Mission

The German Reformed Mission. From this Mission, the Rev. and Mrs. W. E. Hoy were transferred to China last fall; and Miss Hollowell and Mrs. Gill retired from the Mission; so the Mission now comprises 6 families, one single man and two single women, with one married missionary under appointment and expected soon. Dr. and Mrs. Moore have been absent all the year. During the winter, the Rev. and Mrs. H. K. Miller and Miss Rohrbach went to America on furlough; and the Rev. Mr. and Mrs. Lampe and Miss Weidner newly appointed, arrived and are located at Sendai. All the misssionaries on the field at present are located in Sendai; though Mr. Snyder, devoting himself to Bible selling, is absent much of the time.

Japanese assistants

The Mission carries on a High School for girls and one for boys, and also a theological seminary. In the evangelistic work, there are 42 points under its care where the gospel is preached; but at present several places are vacant and more evangelists are needed. Work in two places has been given up through no fault of the Mission. The Mission employs 25 pastors and evangelists, 10 of whom are graduates of their mission academy; and about same number of teachers are employed in the schools, though a number of these give only a part of their time. The Mission appropriated yen 8000 for evangelistic work, and yen 12400 for educational work.

Miyagi Jo Gakko

The girls school, Miyagi Jo Gakko, has during the year been in charge of Miss Zerfluh alone, as Miss Rohrbach's enforced absence because of ill health left her the sole care. The grade of the school is 5 years beyond that of the Higher Primary Schools, with an additional

56

post-graduate year of preparation for Bible work. There have been 48 pupils in regular attendance, and there were 59 in school at the end of April. Five were graduated in June, 1899. There have been 11 baptisms during the year, and there are 35 Christians in school. The school is 12 years old. Of the 21 graduates, 7 are teaching in mission schools, and 3 are Bible women. The amount of mission money expended for the school is *yen* 3881.

The Tohoku Gakuin, the Higher School for boys, is in charge of Dr. Schneder, Mr. Noss and Mr. Gerhard. The grade of the Academic Department corresponds to that of the government Common Middle School ; i.e., it is 5 years beyond of the Higher Primary Schools, with special attention given to English ; and there is an additional two years literary course. There have been 106 pupils in attendance, and there were 96 in school at the end of April, chiefly in the lower classes. There were no graduates last commencement. There were 5 baptisms during the year, and there are 21 Christians in school. Dr. Schneder writes, "Our lower classes are large, but as the young men get on in their course they go into government schools to avoid conscription and get into line of entrance into higher government schools. Our higher classes are very small, or wanting altogether. Altogether, the year has not been a very satisfactory one to us." The school is 14 years old. Of the 51 graduates, 3 are teaching in mission schools, 17 are in evangelistic work in mission employ, and 3 are pastors of self-supporting churches. The cost of the school to the Mission is *yen* 7000.

The Theological Seminary has a vernacular and an English course running parallel, each 3 years long. There were 2 graduates from the English course last commencement. At present, there are only 6 students in the seminary, all in the middle year ; but 3 of them are in the vernacular course and 3 in the English course. These latter are graduates of the Academic Department of the Tohoku Gakuin. Fifteen hours of missionary time each week are given to each class in the English course. There is now but one such class ; so 15 hours represents the amount of missionary time given to the seminary. Mr. Noss says, "The cause of the paucity of students is our reluctance to allow them to take the short cut through the Japanese course, and the impossibility of keeping students in the Academic Department beyond the age when they begin to appreciate the significance of the Christian ministry." He thinks the removal of the government restrictions would result in an increase of theological students. Two of the Japanese professors of theology resigned during the year; and in their places, the Rev. Mr. Kajiwara of Princeton, and the Rev. Mr. Sasao of the University of Bonn, Germany, both of whom have always been identified with the Church of Christ in Japan and are of an evangelistic spirit, have been secured. The seminary costs about *yen* 1000.

Churches

There are four independent churches associated with the Mission. Mr. Noss reports that they have all had a good year. In Sendai, chiefly though the efforts of Dr. Schneder, a beautiful church is building on the most suitable corner lot in the city. The building alone will cost *yen* 12000 ; and of this sum nearly *yen* 2000 were contributed by the Japanese at the cost of commendable self-sacrifice. The churches at Iizaka and Nagaoka have been under the care of one man, a devoted pastor. The latter town is dominated by Christian influence. The Hakodate Christians have repaired their church at a cost of *yen* 500). The work at Wakamatsu has been been carried on by two ordained men working at their own charges ; but recently one of these has been removed to Sendai to be a professor in the Theological Seminary, and the other is sick ; so the Mission will continue the work, and hopes to send an evangelist there. The number of baptisms during the year in the four churches and at Wakamatsu was 76.

Evangelistic work

The evangelistic work of the Mission has been carried on at a disadvantage this year, as there were so few missionaries on the field. Mr. Miller was the only member of the Mission who gave his whole time to evangelistic work ; and after his departure for America, Dr. Schneder and Mr. Noss had, in addition to their heavy school work, the responsibility of the whole evangelistic field which ex-

tends over Miyagi, Yamagata, Akita and Fukushima
Kens, with a part of Saitama Ken, and some work in
Tokyo. Mr. Miller was stationed in Yamagata ; and had
charge of the work there and at Akita, which is three
days' journey distant. Two others of his stations were a
day's journey away and some were nearer. In some of
the stations, the outlook is promising, but the whole district is intensely conservative and hard to move. A railroad is now building which will bring the stations within easier reach, and also it is hoped tend to open the
minds of the people. At Akita, the evangelist left the
work under circumstances which indicated that he was
merely a hireling. The Mission hopes soon to place a
good man there. In the work that is looked after from
Sendai, 12 stations are mentioned, all within a day's journey, and only a few hours away. The evangelists have
worked with commendable zeal and faithfulness, and
gradually are getting to be more practical, and to under-
stand what kind of work will be effective and what not.
There has been special interest at Shiraishi. The great
fire of last year produced such discouraging conditions
that, at that time, the evangelist wanted to give up the
work. Now however a new interest has sprung up, attendance at the services is good, and they have raised money
enough to buy a lot for a new church. In Ishinomaki, a
fine chapel has been built, to which the people contributed
yen 400. In some places, there have been discouragements.
In one, Christians got into trouble by violating the election
laws ; in another, they were mixed up in a fraudulent
life insurance business ; and in yet another, a nominal
believer killed a man in the preaching place itself, pre-
sumably in self-defense. All of these have been set-backs
to the work ; but in all the preaching places under the care
of the Mission, III adults have been baptized during the
year. Mr. Noss says, " There is a marked determination
among the churches and preaching places to purge the church
rolls, and a growing recognition of the fact that it is a mis-
take to baptize unconverted or half converted people. The
Christians are beginning to emphasize the individual aspect

59

of religion instead of the old habit of thinking of it in relation to the welfare of the nation. Audiences are large and respectful wherever we go. The officials are as friendly as they dare be. Our tent meetings, held during the great festivals in Sendai, are better attended than ever; and even the government Boys High School has opened its doors for Christian lectures, and missionaries are frequently asked to address educational associations on the subject of morality and its relation to religion.

Bible selling Mr. Snyder's work of Bible selling has been remarkably successful, about 58000 portions having been sold during the year, in addition to over 1100 Bibles and Testaments. Most of his work has been done on the trains, but he has also sold from house to house, to groups on the street, etc. He finds there are many who really *want* the Word of God, if only we will carry it to them. Mr. Snyder's example and success have also aroused greatly increased efforts in Bible selling with good success on the part of other missionaries, as many of the reports testify.

The year moderately successful In closing our review of the work of the Coöperating Missions, the year may be classed as a moderately successful one. In general, the work has held its own; in some places, fair progress has been made. And after making due allowance for the very evident "professional cheerfulness" characterizing some of the reports, we still find that, on the whole, the condition of the work is to be pronounced "encouraging."

No change in policy Though some years ago the passport system was alleged to be the great barrier to a more active and aggressive pursuance of direct evangelistic work in the country at large, the abolition of that hindrance and the establishing of mixed residence has made no change in the policy of the Missions. No new stations have been opened; a few have been given up or left unoccupied.

Lack of funds Many say that the work in their charge has suffered from lack of oversight which they were unable to give owing to over-pressure of work, or the distance of the fields. Nearly every report of evangelistic work mentions opportunities that had to be left unimproved, or calls for work unanswered. Generally speaking, devices and baits are no longer needed in order to secure hearers for the gospel message. Lack of funds and lack of workers seem to be the chief hindrances to the work now ; The country is open, the people ready to hear, but how shall they hear without a preacher ?

In almost every report the need for more Japanese workers is emphasized, and the question which calls for the most serious consideration of the Council this year, and which can no longer be put aside, is, How can good Japanese workers be obtained for and retained in the work ? It is not that institutions for educating or training are lacking, or that they are deficient in their curricula. The trouble is that the work does not attract our educated youths. There are fewer students in the theological seminaries than for many years past, only 11 in the two institutions ; and the Bible training schools report a falling off in pupils. It is not the fault of the institutions, nor of the advantages and attractions within their walls. It is because the work that lies beyond graduation does not attract. How can we impress upon our Christian youth the need and importance of the direct evangelistic work ? How can we make them realize that this work of preaching the gospel to the heathen, of taking it to the masses of the people in their own neighborhoods and homes, so far from being a mean or insignificant work, is one that offers the greatest scope to a sanctified ambition and, beyond any work in the world, gives opportunities for the use of every power, talent and accomplishment a man may possess ? How can we inspire them with a desire first to fit themselves for, and then to devote their lives to, this most difficult but most exalted work ?

STATISTICS FOR THE YEAR ENDING APRIL 30TH, 1900.*

	Pupils in attendance at the end of April	Number of baptisms	Number of Christians	Whole number of graduates	Graduates last commencement	Graduates teaching in mission schools	Graduates in evangelistic employ of Missions	Cost of school to missions plus missionaries salaries
								Yen
GIRLS BOARDING SCHOOLS								
Sturges Seminary	54	4	13	29	4	1	1	2697
Kinjo Jo Gakko	55	8	16	20	2		3	934
Wilmina "	32		9			3		1300
Hokuriku "	37		22	48	5	5	5	1259
Kojo "	28		13	14	2	6	1	1500
Naniwa "	48		13		4	3	2	2597
Joshi Gakuin	180	3	65	48†	7	19†	5†	2826
Hokusei Jo Gakko	68	5	21	18	1	3		1340
Ferris Seminary	54	4	24	70	3	8	8	5050
Miyagi Jo Gakko	59	11	35	21	5	7	3	3881
Total	261	35	231	270	33	55	28	23693
BOYS BOARDING SCHOOLS								
Steele College	85	3	6	25			4	2670
Meiji Gakuin	80		21	134	6	6	5	4200
Tohoku "	96	5	21	51		3	17	7000
Total	261	8	48	210	6	9	25	13870

* The statistics contained in these tables differ in some particulars from those in the table prepared by the Committee on Statistics (see pages 9–10). This difference is to be accounted for, in part at least, by the fact that the tables were not made up to the same date.

† These figures refer only to the graduates since 1890, the year in which the Joshi Gakuin was formed by uniting Graham Seminary and Sakurai Jo Gakko.

	Pupils in attendance at the end of April	Number of baptisms	Number of Christians	Whole number of graduates	Graduates at last commencement	Graduates teaching in mission schools	Graduates in the evangelistic work of the missions	Cost of school to the Mission plus missionaries salaries
DAY SCHOOLS								
Biwa Shiritsu	53		21		15			625
Kiiku	157							40
Seishi	90							120
Keimo Nos. 1 & 2	130							600
KINDERGARTENS								
Kanazawa	20							
Shinagawa	40							200
Nishijin	38							
Margaret Ayres	43							
BIBLE WOMEN'S SCHOOLS								
Tra Training Sch.	8	5		9	1	3	6	1142
Seisho Gakuin	13			50	2	3	20	
Ferris Sem. Bible Course	1							

63

STATISTICS OF THE YEAR ENDING APRIL 30TH, 1900.
(CONTINUED)

THEO. SEMINARIES	Students in attendance at end of April	Whole number of graduates	Graduates at last commencement	Cost to missions plus missionaries salaries
Meiji Gakuin	5	143*	2	yen 2540
Tohoku Gakuin	6	33†	2	1000
Total	11	176	4	3540

MISSION STATISTICS.

	No. pastors and evangelists	Graduates Academic Dpt. mission schools	Appropriations for evangelistic work	Appropriations for educational work
South Japan Reformed	16	2	yen 5848	yen 4645
Southern Presbyterian	15	4	3020	929
Cumb. Presbyterian	11	2	2000	1200
West Japan Presbyterian	25	14	9482	6457
East Japan Presbyterian	23	1	7377	9922
North Japan Reformed	16		5648	8405
German Reformed	25	10	9000	12400
Total	131	33	41375	43958

* Of these, 73 are now in the service of the Church of Christ in Japan, and 12 in that of other evangelical Churches. Eight (4 of whom are included in the 73) are teachers in Christian schools. Eleven are teachers in government or other schools. Eleven have died; 15 are in other callings; of 12, the Meiji Gakuin has no knowledge.

† Of these, 20 are pastors or evangelists; 2, though supporting themselves by other work, preach statedly; 3 are teachers in the Tohoku Gakuin; 3 are studying in America with a view to doing Christian work or their return; 3 are teaching English in government schools; 1 has given up his faith and 1 has died.

As the Theo. Dept. of Steele College is discontinued for the present, it does not appear in this table. It, with the Theo. School of which it is the successor, numbers 57 graduates. Of these, 24 are still engaged in the work; 3 have died; the rest have retired from the work of their own accord, or have been dropped by the Missions, in some cases because of reductions in the grants of funds made by the Boards.

64

SUPPLEMENT.

The following questions concerning conditions on the evangelistic field were sent to every member of the Co-operating Missions engaged in direct evangelistic work. Forty-one sets of replies were received. These have been edited and classified as well as they could be; and the answers to each question are given herewith. The numbers refer to the names of the writers as indicated in the following list.

1. Dr. Stout.
2. Mr. Oltmans.
3. Mr. Price.
4. Mrs. Price.
5. Mr. McIlvaine.
6. Mr. McAlpine.
7. Mr. Myers.
8. Miss Patton.
9. Mr. Moore.
10. Mr. Cumming.
11. Mr. S. P. Fulton.
12. Mr. W. McS. Buchanan.
13. Miss Leavitt.
14. Mrs. Drennan.
15. Dr. J. B. Hail.
16. Dr. A. D. Hail.
17. Mr. Hudson.
18. Miss Morgan.
19. Mr. Brokaw.
20. Mr. Haworth.
21. Mr. Winn.
22. Mr. Dunlop.

23. { Mr. Curtis.
     { Mr. Ayres.
     { Miss Bigelow.
24. Mr. Jones.
25. Mrs. Jones.
26. Mr. Doughty.
27. Dr. Imbrie.
28. Mr. Pierson.
29. Miss West.
30. Mr. J. H. Ballagh.
31. Mr. Scudder.
32. Mrs. Schenck.
33. Mr. E. R. Miller.
34. Mr. Harris.
35. Mr. H. K. Miller.
36. Dr. Schneder.
37. Mr. Snyder.
38. Mr. Noss.
39. Miss Deyo.
40. Mr. & Mrs. Davidson.
41. Miss Pratt.

1. *Do you find the conditions obtaining under the new treaties and regulations equally or more or less favorable to evangelistic work than were the former conditions ?*

Twenty-four report no practical change (1, 5, 7, 8, 9, 10, 11, 13, 14, 17, 18, 19, 20, 23, 24, 25, 27, 28, 29, 30, 33, 35, 40, 41). Seven report the conditions more favorable (12, 15, 21, 31, 32, 36, 37). Three report the conditions more favorable because of wider conceptions of the people, and the realization that Christianity has an acknowledged position in the country (2, 22, 34). One reports the conditions more favorable as concerns renting of chapels, abolition of the passport system, and the acceptance of the foreign missionary as an inevitable part of the new order of things (16). One observes that missionaries are raised in the estimation of the people, more kindly treated by officials and prominent citizens ; and that there is general recognition of the fact that Christianity can no longer be ignored (38). Three say that missionaries can travel more freely ; but that street-preaching and the opening of new work is more difficult, (3, 4, 6). One writes that street-preaching and preaching in chapels opening on the street are forbidden ; and that vexatious regulations as to the recording of preaching places are in operation (26.) Thirty-two *vs.* six regard the conditions as equally or more favorable.

2. *In view of present conditions would you advocate a wider scattering of missionaries: i.e. that there be only one missionary family in a station and that stations be multiplied?*

Two say, No : one adding, I believe in concentration (23, 4). Four say, Cannot make a change in our field (1, 15, 29, 35). Four say, Not with the present force ; feasible if the force is increased (2, 8, 10, 16). One says, Scatter them if you have them to scatter (33). Three say, Too hard on a family ; two families are better than one, but to more effectively cover the field there might be more scattering (11, 12, 40.) One says, Yes, but young ladies should not be sent out alone (14). Two say,

Yes, for the missionary is the centre of permanent influence and the more stations we have the better. I would advocate one family and one single lady in a station (18, 39). Eight say, I advocate the opening of new stations and the locating of missionaries in unoccupied fields, thus making new centres; but I would not insist upon only one family in a station (3, 5, 6, 13, 17, 20, 21, 41). One says, I believe two families are better than one, if in harmony; but I would advocate a wider scattering of the missionaries now in the treaty ports (26). Yes: because, until foreign missionaries live and work and establish working bodies in the interior towns not much will be accomplished in the way of reaching the masses or establishing self-propagating churches; for the Japanese workers have not as yet enough power of initiative to get a good work started (19). Two say, There should not be less than two families in one place; but if another Mission is represented, then one of the Council missionaries is sufficient; and as many places should be occupied as possible (36, 37). One says, A number of new stations should be permanently occupied by the Council; but that must be done by reënforcements from home, not by a general scattering of the force now in Japan. Nor is it wise as a rule to isolate either individuals or families, unless it be for limited periods of time. Much might be done towards the accomplishment of the purpose underlying the question, especially in places of secondary importance, by adopting some such plan as that successfully pursued a number of years ago by the Joshi Gakuin in connection with Takata: i.e. by having a sufficient force in the educational institutions to enable the institutions, as an important part of their work, to detach individuals in turn to do evangelistic work regularly at certain fixed centres for several months at a time. Such a plan provides a moveable force; avoids continuous isolation; and by dispensing with the necessity of multiplying houses suitable for permanent residence, is relatively inexpensive. In the case of the Joshi Gakuin, it gave to the ladies a profitable, effective and pleasant change of work; and was in many ways of great value to the institution itself. The plan was given up for the lack of force and funds (27). One says, The increase of railroads has on the one hand lessened the necessity for multiplying stations, and on the other diminished the isolation of the lone missionary in a station. I would advocate one or two families in a station and believe that in order to fit missionaries for the general supervision of evangelists, it is necessary that they should serve out an apprenticeship in the direct work (38). Two say, Divide forces and cover territory ; the presence of the missionary adds much to the success of the work anywhere (7, 30). Two say, Yes, emphatically (9, 28). Two say, One family is better than more, but I would not urge it on those who find the isolation very trying (24, 25). Three say, I would advocate one family in a station. If the twenty fields of strategic importance as located by the committee of the Council were supplied at the expense of the treaty ports, we could hope for a speedier and more effective evangelization of the country than by the present arrangement. The missionary should be seen by the people, learn to realize the needs of the people, and personally push the work of evangelization (31, 32, 34).

3. *In your opinion, what proportion of the population of your field has heard, or in any way become acquainted with, the foundation truths of the gospel?*

In general those to whom the questions were sent do not answer ; saying that it would be mere guess work. Those who do venture at a guess vary in their answers from one in ten to one in ten thousand.

4. *Would you say that most emphatically now is the time for more pushing, aggressive evangelistic work?*

Seven say, No more than at any other time (1, 13, 19, 26, 40, 41). Nineteen say, Yes, now as always (3, 4, 5, 8, 9, 10, 11, 15, 16, 17, 18, 20, 21, 22, 29, 33, 35, 38). Two say, Yes ; for every year lost makes the work more difficult, for civilization without Christianity hardens the hearts of the people (7, 39). Nine say, Recently conditions have been growing more favorable, and work should be pushed to the utmost (12, 14, 24, 25, 28, 30, 31, 32, 37). One says, Now is the time to lay foundations carefully by introducing such methods as shall secure stability to the work (2). One says, Yes; and to this end the number of foreign and Japanese workers should be doubled. But we can not hope that the country will be christianized in one great rush; several generations of faithful missionaries will still be needed (36). One says, Yes, by all means; the people are ready to welcome all well directed efforts; the country is agitated over the prevalent immorality and the newspapers and prominent men cry out for reform. In religious matters Japan is now at sea. Christianity has passed its trial stage and shown its ability to satisfy the desires of those who really long for something better. We ought to be fully awake to the present needs and opportunities (34). One says, When I remember the great congregations that once pressed into theatres and other large buildings to hear the truths of Christianity, and when I think that God may have in store for Japan other like days of his presence, I am constrained to say that to-day is emphatically *a* time, rather than emphatically *the* time, to press evangelistic work. Moreover, what we commonly call direct evangelistic work should not be pressed to the lessening or the undervaluing of other forms of Christian effort, and in particular of that form which we usually classify as educational. Christ sent Paul to preach the gospel, and Paul determined not to know anything save Jesus Christ and him crucified; yet Paul made it also a rule of his ministry to become *all* things to *all* men that he might by *all* means save *some*. We should do likewise; and especially so remembering that there are diversities of gifts, but the same Spirit (27.)

5. *If any, how many of the out-stations under your care are more than a day's journey from your place of residence? How many are about a day's journey?*

In answer to this question some have used the word "some" or "several" in place of a definite number. Adding the definite numbers given, it appears that at least

61 out-stations are a day's journey, that 35 are more than a day's journey; while besides these a number are more than two days' journey from the missionary in charge.

6. Provided there were workers enough, would you think it practicable to divide your field, both city and country villages, into districts of say 200 houses each and to hold a series of weekly meetings for children and adults in each district, leaving tracts at each house, etc., and so take the gospel to the people?

Four say, The scarcity of workers makes the question not worth considering (1, 19, 23, 26). Seven say, Yes; (5, 8, 9, 20, 25, 40, 41). Seven say, Yes, if the workers would do the work (2, 6, 11, 22, 24, 29, 30). Two say, Not practicable. (13, 17). Neither practicable nor effective (33). One says, As a question, purely hypothetical, since there are not workers enough to make the attempt: as a method, considering the quality as well as the size of the army necessary for such an campaign, visionary : as an idea, apparently superficial in its conception of what taking the gospel to a people really means (27). Two say, it depends on circumstances (16, 21). Three say, Perfectly practicable (15, 28, 32). Five say, Effective if practicable (4, 7, 10, 18, 37). Five would like to see the country districted and every house visited (3, 31, 34, 36, 39). Two already have this plan under contemplation (12, 14). One says, Practicable with comity (38). One says, I see no reason why it could not be done; it would be the best way to reach all classes and to find out the real state of the people, and would greatly tend to the progress of the work (34).

7. Do you think that more could be done on the field in general in the way of organizing and training local bands of volunteer workers from among the Christians connected with the churches and preaching places?

Nine say, Yes, (10, 11, 12, 16, 18, 20, 25, 28, 29). Two say, Doubtful (1, 14). One says, Not in our field (8). Three say, Yes, when there is some one with an organizing faculty (33, 38, 40). Four say, Desirable, but it depends upon the coöperation of the Japanese (2, 3, 17, 34) Two say, Possible where there is missionary oversight (30, 36). Seven say, Desirable and possible ; a great deal more could be done (6, 7, 13, 21, 22, 35, 41). Yes, but care must be taken not to supersede the regular evangelists (9). Can be done and ought to be done ; but the system of having paid workers is detrimental to such a plan (5). Yes, and I recommend the Nevius plan (23). It is not the place of the missionary to organize ; purely advisory relations are all that he has any right to exercise (26). Desirable, but rendered difficult by the nomadic character of the Church members (32). Two say, Should be pushed with all our power, not only for the sake of evangelization but for the sake of the Christians themselves ; their spiritual life is atrophying for the lack of exercise (19, 39). One says, Personal effort for others if wisely exerted is of the very highest value, and everything possible should done to quicken and to foster it. The question contemplates something more : the organization and training of volunteer bands. At certain times, in certain places, for certain persons, such a work is comparatively easy to begin ; the difficulty is to keep it up. No doubt however more might be done by wisely directed effort ; but in any case it should be regarded as a method supplementary to that of a ministry that lives of the gospel ; and special pains should be taken to cultivate in the volunteers preëminence in love, rather than the love of preëminence (27). Five say, Possible and necessary (4, 15, 24, 31, 37). One adds, Because the Christians are willing ; the security of the Church depends upon its getting beyond self and working for others ; the country can not be evangelized by paid workers only (31).

8. *Are the mission school' graduates, men and women, living within the boundaries of your field, but not in mission employ, active Christian workers? is their influence actively exerted for Christ and the Church?*

Five have had no opportunities for observation (10, 21, 29, 34, 35). Five say, Not the extent we ought to expect

71

(1, 31, 32, 33, 41). One says, Taking the whole field occupied by our Mission in view, not to the extent we ought to expect. In the Wakayama field, we have no graduates from mission schools excepting our pastors and two men in government employ. The two men in government employ are active Christians and use their influence for Christ. The graduates of the schools for girls, so far as I know, are all Christian workers in the sense that their influence is exerted for Christ (15). Two say, Not to the extent that we wish, but as much so as we have a right to expect (38). One says, Not so much so as we wish; and it may be that it is partly our own fault. But let us remember that they are in the midst of an environment whose difficulties and perils no one of us really knows. It is not strange that many of them, and many others too some of whom have run long and well, should love this present world. Yet there are many of our graduates, especially perhaps among those from our schools for girls, who are letting their light shine; some who are pressing on toward the goal for the prize. For all such Paul said, I thank my God always (27). Four say, There are both kinds; much depends upon the surroundings (2, 18, 23, 40). Two know of none such in their fields (17, 30). Two know of none such, but know of several who do Christian work (5, 25). Four say, There are more in hiding than are actively exerting a Christian influence (3, 4, 24, 39). Four say, Those whom I know are excellent (8, 13, 19, 26). Three say, With few exceptions they are (20, 28, 37). Two know only one, and he is not a Christian (11, 12). Not many here; those who are not connected with the Chu Gakko are the best workers in this field (7). Some of our best and most influential workers are from mission schools. A few have been flat failures (16). With few exceptions they are of no benefit at all to the work (9). I know only one, a former preacher; and his influence is against Christianity (14). I can hardly say that their influence is actively and openly exerted for Christ and the Church; but I believe that their secret influence is good (22). Some are really decent Christians; others are, well, moderate, very moderate (6).

9. *Is it your experience that those among your Christians and inquirers who have been led to Christianity by means of English classes, etc., continue their interest and zeal after the English instruction is discontinued?*

Twelve have no experience (1, 5, 17, 18, 20, 24, 28, 29, 35, 37, 40, 41). One says, I have myself no experience, for I do not remember to have ever led a single soul to Christ through the use of English; and I do not *know* of many who have been led to Christ by means of English classes; but of those I do know, some have made earnest Christians and some have not (15). Three say, No, they do not (9, 13, 25). Two say, Yes, they do (7, 8). Three say, A few (4, 16, 38). Two say, Most do not (23, 30). Eight say, As much so as the average (3, 6, 11, 12, 14, 21, 22, 27). One says, English classes serve as a good introduction, but in themselves fail of good results (33, 36). Those who become Christians keep up their interest, but the results of English classes are not large (19). Two say, English classes are a delusion and a snare, and are responsible for much hypocrisy. Doubtless some good Christians come out of these classes, but they are few (26, 39). Five say, Teaching only the Bible in English is productive of good results (2, 10, 31, 32, 34).

10. *Would you think it practicable for the missionary to have employed under him on a salary, young men lay-workers as a sort of shosei (pupils, scholars), in the same way in which young women are employed under lady missionaries? The young men to be looking forward to entering the Theological Seminary and the ministry or not, as the case may be; their duty while with the missionary being to work with him, especially in meetings for boys and young men.*

Three say, Cannot say (8, 13, 18). Three say, Difficult (7, 16, 23). Six say, No (12, 17, 19, 21, 36, 38). Seven say, Yes (20, 24, 25, 28, 32, 40, 41). Two say, Have tried it once and would not like to try it again (1, 26).

73

Four say, It would work mischief (2, 4, 33, 37). Five say, Liable to abuse but desirable if possible (3, 11, 30, 31 39). Three say, It might be good in some places, but not good for general adoption (10, 22, 29). One says, It might work well in some cases; but it is not without its dangers. The Church of Christ in Japan needs to raise up a ministry that lives of the gospel; but the general adoption of the plan suggested, with its numerous groups of young men on a salary and some of them without even a fixed purpose of entering the ministry, would tend to the growth of a laity that would live of the Missions (27.) Practicable but detrimental to volunteer workers (5). Such workers should be volunteers (6). Should always be done for at least two years before going to the Theological Seminary (9). Have tried it for ten years with excellent results (14). Practicable but not desirable (15). Practicable and a fine thing; rather a new departure, but we need new methods (34). Quite in line with the patron system of Japan and worth trying (35).

11. Do you think the time has come when the institutional church could wisely be established as an evangelizing agency in Japan?

Five say, If done at all, it should be done by the Japanese (2, 17, 19, 25, 35). Fourteen say, No (1, 4, 10, 11, 12, 21, 22, 23, 26, 28, 36, 38, 40, 41). Nine say, Do not know (5, 19, 13, 15, 18, 24, 29, 30, 37). Two say, Yes (14, 20). One says, I think the institutional church the ideal for all churches always under all circumstances, when modified to suit the surroundings (16). Two favor the general idea if separated from the place of worship (3, 7). Six favor trying to have the church provide a pleasant gathering place, where leisure time can be profitably employed by those whose home surroundings are not conducive to growth in grace (6, 31, 32, 33, 34, 39). One says, I have no intention at present of establishing an institutional church myself; but if any one is fully persuaded in his own mind, knows how to do it and has the funds, I will hold his hat (27).

III.

ROLL OF THE COUNCIL.

EAST JAPAN MISSION OF THE PRESBYTERIAN
CHURCH IN THE U. S. A. (NORTHERN).

Ballagh, Mr. J.C.,* 1875† . . . . . . Tokyo.
Ballagh, Mrs. J.C., 1884 . . . (in U.S.) , ,,
Haworth, Rev. B.C.,* 1887 . . . . . ,,
Haworth, Mrs. B.C.*. . . . . ,,
Imbrie, Rev. William, D.D.,* 1875 . . . ,,
Imbrie, Mrs. William . . . . ,,
Landis, Rev. H.M.,* 1888 . . . . . . ,,
Landis, Mrs. H.M.* . . . . ,,
MacNair, Rev. T.M.,* 1883 . . . . . ,,
MacNair, Mrs. T.M.,* 1880 . . . . . ,,
Pierson, Rev. G.P., 1888 . . . . . . Sapporo.
Pierson, Mrs. G.P., 1891 . . . . . . ,,
Thompson, Rev. David, D.D., 1863 . . . Tokyo.
Thompson, Mrs. David, 1873 . . . . . ,,

Ballagh, Miss A.P., 1884 . . . . . . ,,
Case, Miss E.W.,* 1887 . . . . . . Yokohama.
Davis, Miss A.K., 1880 . . . (in U.S.) Tokyo.
Gardner, Miss Sarah, 1889 . . . . . ,,
McCauley, Mrs. J.K.,* 1880 . . . . . ,,

* Present at the meeting of the Council in Karuizawa, July, 1900.
† Year of arrrival in Japan.

Milliken, Miss Elizabeth P., 1884. (in U.S.) Tokyo.
Rose, Miss C.II., 1886 . . . . Otaru.
Smith, Miss S.C., 1880 . . . . Sapporo.
Wells, Miss Lilian, 1900 . . . . . . „
West, Miss A.B., 1883 . . . . Tokyo.
Youngman, Miss K.M., 1873 . . . . „

WEST JAPAN MISSION OF THE PRESBYTERIAN
CHURCH IN THE U. S. A. (NORTHERN).

Alexander, Rev. T.T., D.D., 1877 . . . Kyoto.
Alexander, Mrs. T.T. . . . . (in U.S.) „
Ayres, Rev. J.B., 1888 . . . . Yamaguchi.
Ayres, Mrs. J.B. . . . . „
Brokaw, Rev. H.,* 1896 . . . . . . Hiroshima.
Brokaw, Mrs. H.* . . . . „
Bryan, Rev. A.V., 1882 . . . (in U.S.) Osaka.
Bryan, Mrs. A.V., 1887 . . . („ „) „
Curtis, Rev. F.S., 1887 . . . . . . Yamaguchi.
Curtis, Mrs. F.S. . . . . „
Doughty, Rev. J.W., 1890 . . . . . . Hiroshima.
Doughty, Mrs. J.W. . . . . „
Dunlop, Rev. J.G. 1890 . . . . . . Kanazawa.
Dunlop, Mrs. J.G., 1894 . . . . . . „
Fulton, Rev. G.W., 1889 . . . . . . „
Fulton, Mrs. G.W. . . . . „
Jones, Rev. W.Y.,* 1895 . . . . . . Fukui.
Jones, Mrs. W.Y.,* 1884 . . . . . . „
Porter, Rev. J.B., 1881 . . . (in U.S.) Kyoto.
Porter, Mrs. J.B., 1884 . . . („ „) „
Winn, Rev. T.C.,* 1878 . . . . . . Osaka.
Winn, Mrs. T.C.* . . . . „

Bigelow, Miss G.S., 1886 . . . . . . Yamaguchi.
Garvin, Miss A.E., 1882 . . . . . . Osaka.
Glenn, Miss Grace Curtis* 1898 . . . Kanazawa.
Kelly, Miss M.E., 1893 . . . . Kyoto.
Luther, Miss Ida R.,* 1898 . . . . . Kanazawa.
Palmer, Miss M.M., 1892 . . . (in U.S.) Yamaguchi.

Porter, Miss F.E., 1882 . . . (in U.S.) Kanazawa.
Settlemeyer, Miss E.,* 1893 . . . . . Kyoto.
Shaw, Miss Kate,* 1889 . . . . . . Kanazawa.

NORTH JAPAN MISSION OF THE REFORMED (DUTCH) CHURCH IN AMERICA.

Ballagh, Rev. J.H.,* 1861 . . . . . Yokohama.
Ballagh, Mrs. J.H.* . . . . „
Booth, Rev. Eugene S.,* 1879 . . . . „
Booth, Mrs. Eugene S.* . . . . . . „
Harris, Rev. Howard, 1883 . . . . . Aomori.
Harris, Mrs. Howard . . . . „
Miller, Rev. E. Rothesay,* 1872 . . . . Morioka.
Miller, Mrs. E. Rothesay,* 1870 . . . . „
Scudder, Rev. Frank S.,* 1897 . . . . Nagano.
Scudder, Mrs. Frank S.* . . . . . . „
Wyckoff, M.N., D.Sc.,* 1881 . . . . . Tokyo.
Wyckoff, Mrs. M.N.* . . . . „

Deyo, Miss Mary,* 1888 . . . (in U.S.) Ueda.
Moulton, Miss Julia, 1891 . . . . . Yokohama.
Schenck, Mrs. J.W.,* 1897 . . . . . Nagano.
Thompson, Miss Anne De F., 1887. (in U.S.) Yokohama.
Winn, Miss L., 1881 . . . .(„ „) Aomori.
Wyckoff, Miss Harriet J.,* 1898 . . . Yokohama.

SOUTH JAPAN MISSION OF THE REFORMED (DUTCH) CHURCH IN AMERICA.

Myers, Rev. C.M., 1899 . . . . . . Nagasaki.
Oltmans, Rev. Albert, 1886 . . . . . Saga.
Oltmans, Mrs. Albert . . . . . . „
Peeke, Rev. H.V.S.,* 1893 . . . . . Kagoshima.
Peeke, Mrs. H.V.S.* . . . . . . „
Pieters, Rev. Albertus, 1891 . . (in U.S.) „
Pieters, Mrs. Albertus . . . .(„ „) „
Stout, Rev. Henry, D.D., 1869 . . . . Nagasaki.
Stout, Mrs. Henry . . . . „

77

Couch, Miss Sara M., 1892 . . (in U.S.) Nagasaki.
Lansing, Miss Harriet M., 1893 . . . . Kagoshima.
Stout, Miss A.B., 1898 . . . . Nagasaki.
Stryker, Miss A.K., 1897 . . . . . .   „

MISSION OF THE UNITED PRESBYTERIAN
CHURCH OF SCOTLAND.

Davidson, Rev. Robert Y.,* 1874 . . . Tokyo.
Davidson, Mrs. Robert Y.,* 1877 . . .   „
Waddell, Rev. Hugh, 1874. . (in Ireland)   „
Waddell, Mrs. Hugh, 1896. . („   „)   „

MISSION OF THE PRESBYTERIAN CHURCH
IN THE U. S. (SOUTHERN).

Buchanan, Rev. W.C., 1891 . . (in U.S.) Takamatsu.
Buchanan, Mrs. W.C. . . . .(„   „)   „
Buchanan, Rev. Walter McS., 1895 . .   „
Buchanan, Mrs. Walter McS., 1887 . .   „
Cumming, Rev. C.K., 1889 . . . . . Nagoya.
Cumming, Mrs. C.K., 1892 . . . . .   „
Fulton, Rev. S.P., 1888 . . . . . . Okazaki.
Fulton, Mrs. S.P. . . . .   „
Hope, Rev. S.R., 1892 . . . .(in U.S.) Tokushima.
Hope, Mrs. S.R. . . . . . .(„   „)   „
McAlpine, Rev. R.E., 1885 . . . . . Nagoya.
McAlpine, Mrs. R.E. . . . .   „
McIlvaine, Rev. W.B.,* 1889 . . . . Kochi.
McIlvaine, Mrs. W.B. . . . .   „
Moore, Rev. J.B.,* 1890 . . . . . . Susaki.
Moore, Mrs. J.B., 1893 . . . . . .   „
Myers, Rev. H.W., 1897 . . . . . . Tokushima.
Myers, Mrs. H.W. . . . .   „
Price, Rev. H.B., 1887 . . . . Kobe.
Price, Mrs. H.B., 1890 . . . .   „

Dowd, Miss Annie,* 1887 . . . . . .   „
Evans, Miss Sala, 1893 . . .(in U.S.) Kochi.

78

Houston, Miss Ella, 1891 . . . („ „) Nagoya.
Moore, Miss Elizabeth, 1894 . . . . . „
Patton, Miss Florence, 1895 . . . . . Tokushima.
Sterling, Miss Charlotte E., 1887 . (in U.S.) Kochi.
Wimbish, Miss Elizabeth, 1887 . . . . Nagoya.

MISSION OF THE REFORMED (GERMAN) CHURCH IN THE U. S.

Faust, Rev. A.K., 1900 . . . . . . Sendai.
Faust, Mrs. A.K. . . . . „
Gerhard, Mr. Paul L.,* 1897 . . . . . „
Lampe, Rev. W.E.,* 1900 . . . . . „
Lampe, Mrs. W.E. . . . . „
Miller, Rev. H.K., 1892 . . . (in U.S.) Yamagata.
Miller, Mrs. H.K. . . . . . („ „) „
Moore, Rev. J.P., D.D., 1883 . . { „ „) Tokyo.
Moore, Mrs. J.P. . . . . . („ „) „
Noss, Rev. C., 1895 . . . . Sendai.
Noss, Mrs. C. . . . . „
Schneder, Rev. D.B., D.D., 1887 . . . „
Schneder, Mrs. D.B. . . . . . . „
Snyder, Rev. S.S.,* 1894 . . . . . . „
Snyder, Mrs. S.S. . . . . „

Powell, Miss Lucy M., 1900 . . . . . „
Rohrbach, Miss Lillie May, 1894 . . . „
Weidner, Miss Sadie Lea,* 1900 . . . „
Zurfluh, Miss Lena, 1894 . . . . . . „

MISSION OF THE CUMBERLAND PRESBYTERIAN CHURCH.

Hail, Rev. A.D., D.D., 1878 . . . . . Osaka.
Hail, Mrs. A.D. . . . . „
Hail, Rev. J.B., D.D.,* 1877 . . . . . Wakayama.
Hail, Mrs. J.B. . . . . „
Hail, Rev. J.E., 1900 . . . .
Worley, Rev. J.C., 1899 . . . . . . Tsu, Ise.

```
Worley, Mrs. J.C. . . . . . . . .    Tsu, Ise.
Hudson, Rev. G.G., 1886 . . . . . .  Osaka.
Hudson, Mrs. G.G. . . . . . . . .       „
Van Horne, Rev. G.W., 1888 . (in U.S.)  „
Van Horne, Mrs. G.W. . . . ( „  „ )     „

Alexander, Miss S., 1894. . . . ( „  „ )  Takatsuki.
Drennan, Mrs. A.M., 1883 . . . . .   Tsu, Ise.
Gardner, Miss Ella, 1893 . . . . . .  Osaka.
Leavitt, Miss Julia, 1881 . . . . . .  Tanabe.
Lyons, Mrs. N.A., 1894 . . . . . .  Osaka.
Morgan, Miss Agnes E., 1889 . . . .     „
```

WOMANS UNION MISSIONARY SOCIETY.

```
Crosby, Miss Julia N., 1871 . . . . .  Yokohama.
Pratt, Miss S.A., 1893 . . . . . . .      „
```